I0580979

MONTEREY KING

CALIFORNIA SUITS, BOOK THREE

CLAIRE MARTI

MONTEREY KING, California Suits, Book Three

Copyright © 2022 by Claire Marti

ISBN: eBook 978-1-7372993-4-9

ISBN: Paperback 978-1-7372993-5-6

Published By: Claire Marti

Editor: Lindsey Faber

Proofreader: Shasta Shafer

Cover Design: Christina Hovland

❈ Created with Vellum

For Josie--the sweetest dog to bless this earth!

CHAPTER 1

*L*ucy Goodwin despised Mondays. Always had.

When she was a little girl, Mondays were spent in sterile hospital rooms. When she was twenty years old, a Monday in August marked the day her heart broke. When she'd woken up this morning, she resolved this Monday would be different. This Monday she would conquer the first day of her dream job as wedding planner for Cypress Coast Ranch.

The upcoming pitch meeting with the wealthy heiress who had publicly scorned every other wedding venue from Seattle to San Diego to her ten million social media followers? Piece of cake––Lucy would win the contract.

The Hotel Kings, LLC, Vice President of Sales and Marketing and CEO sitting in on the meeting and assessing her skills after her hasty hiring just last week? Easy peasy–– Lucy excelled under pressure.

But sharing the conference table with the hotel's Managing Director, Cameron Taylor, who she hadn't set eyes on since he'd dumped her thirteen years ago? Yeah, that explained why her pulse pounded in her temples like the massive surf crashing on the nearby Monterey shore. She paused in front of the closed conference room door, taking a moment to gather her composure.

"The door isn't locked." An unmistakable voice rasped from beside her.

She spun around and her throat tightened the moment her eyes locked with Cameron Taylor's arctic blue gaze.

How could someone look so familiar yet like a stranger? Lucy studied his lean, angular face. His strong, slightly crooked nose was the same, as was the determined square-ness of his jawline. Small lines fanned out from his arresting eyes and grooves bracketed his chiseled mouth, which was pressed into a firm line. His posture was ramrod straight––even more rigid after a dozen years serving overseas in the Army.

"Cam." How many times had she imagined what she'd say if she ever saw him again? How many impassioned speeches had she rehearsed before moving on with her life?

He inclined his head. "Hi, Lucy." His crisp tone was as remote as his stony expression. The voice of an acquaintance––not the man she'd shared the love of a lifetime with until he'd broken her heart.

Through impeccable self-control, if she did say so herself, she forced her lips to curve upward. "So... how are you?" Awkward, but it was the best she had to offer. She hadn't expected to encounter him one-on-one, at least not yet.

"Fine, but we should go in. Ryan and Charlie are waiting." Cam reached for the mahogany wooden door's carved brass handle at the same time she did.

His long, blunt fingers brushed hers. A flash of heat sparked up her arm and she snatched her hand back. Muscle memory? Of course, Mr. Poker Face didn't flinch as he pushed the large door open.

Bright light flooded the conference room and bathed the expansive space in a golden glow. Lucy blinked. January on the Monterey coastline wasn't celebrated for clear blue skies, but the cloudy gray morning had cleared, and rays of sunshine exposed the rugged Pacific coastline beyond the floor-to-ceiling windows.

"Lucy, Cam, there you both are. Come on in." Charlotte "Charlie" Ray, the Vice President of Sales and Marketing for the luxury boutique hotel chain, flashed her gleaming white smile and waved a slender hand. The tall, elegant blonde was driven, passionate, and friendly. They'd connected immediately during the interview to fill the in-house wedding planner position her friend Joy had bailed on last-minute.

Charlie sat next to her fiancé Ryan Michaels, the Hotel Kings CEO, at the head of a long rustic oak table. Lucy and Ryan had been friends once, back when he was simply one of Cam's college buddies. Now he was running the business the guys had dreamt up after a grueling ROTC summer session.

Lucy's death grip on her daffodil-colored briefcase softened. Before the morning was over, she'd clinch the wedding of the century, impress the heck out of Ryan and Charlie, and make Cameron Taylor burn with regret. And her Monday curse would be resolved.

Go time.

She strode toward the table, a smile on her face. "Good morning. Thanks for bringing the San Diego weather with you. It's a positive sign we'll secure the Harrington wedding, right?"

"I like the way you think. This deal will literally put Cypress Coast Ranch on the map. No pressure." Charlie grinned.

Cam coughed and pulled out a chair at the far end of the table.

Ryan, a handsome, golden-haired, blue-eyed guy, smiled.

"Lucy, it's been too long. We're lucky you could step in at the last minute. Otherwise, Charlie would be flying up here constantly and I need her in La Jolla."

Lucy tilted her head and focused on Ryan. "It's so great to see you guys followed through with starting your business together. I'm excited to be a part of it." Although working with the one man who'd broken her heart wasn't exactly how she'd define getting lucky.

Ryan, his younger brother Austin, and his three college buddies, Cam, Jack, and Lucas had recently started the new hotel chain. Lucy remembered the guys as a loyal band of brothers but hadn't expected to see any of them again after she and Cam broke up. Apparently, the universe had other plans.

Determined not to let Cam's presence ruffle her composure, Lucy unpacked her sleek laptop and 3-ring emerald green binder. Fortunately, Cam sat far enough away she could ignore him. If simply seeing him shook her to her core, she definitely needed distance. Especially from another hint of his beachy, clean scent, like she'd caught in the doorway. *Dangerous.*

Tonight, she'd have plenty of time to obsess over her thundering heartbeat and the slight trembling of her fingers. To contemplate Cam's icy reserve. Now wasn't the time to reflect on the unexpected surge of memories.

Ryan cleared his throat. "We've only got about forty-five minutes before the Harringtons arrive and I'm headed off to another meeting. Lucy, would you run through your pitch for us?"

She nodded and opened the PowerPoint presentation she'd tweaked and polished until 2 a.m. "Absolutely. So, I have some slides, and based on my research on Victoria, she's not going to be able to sit still and focus on a screen. But her mother wants the formal pitch and she's footing the bill. It will launch us into the tour."

Charlie nodded. "Excellent––Victoria will have to fall in love with the venue and us, but if her mother doesn't approve, she'll nix the deal."

"Exactly. So, we start here and make them feel important because the executive team of the hotel chain took the time to say hello and welcome them. We're pulling out all the stops up front."

Today was a pivotal day for her career and for Cypress Coast Ranch's position as the new "it" wedding destination on the Monterey Peninsula. Competition was stiff with the Pebble Beach Resort close by and other luxury hotels with established clientele.

"Great," Ryan said.

Cam remained silent. Good, because the sound of his low, husky voice could derail her focus, which wasn't an option. No time for distractions.

"Once we've finished the meet and greet, I'll give a quick overview of what we can do for them that nobody else can." She ticked the items off her fingers. "We will reserve the entire resort for her special day, ensuring her privacy and exclusivity. We'll work with her to implement her vision–– the ceremony, the flowers, the theme, the reception, the music, the chef. Anything she requires from recommendations for the designer to create her gown to a hair and make-up team––we've got it.

"She wants as much of the wedding and reception outdoors as possible, so we'll be creating a dance floor for her, tents, and whatever else, depending upon the theme she selects." Lucy scrolled through the slides until she found the ones where she'd created different layouts for the gardens and the resort's private beach.

She angled her screen toward them, then passed out the hard copies, careful to avoid Cam's gaze. "Here are a few options I thought would suit her best."

Lucy nibbled on the inside of her cheek while they flipped through the pages, eager for their reaction. Although she was confident in her abilities, she couldn't afford to not land this prestigious client. Once she'd demonstrated her genuine passion and mad skills, any remaining trepidation they might harbor over her last-minute hiring would drift away on tendrils of Monterey morning fog.

"These are great, Lucy." Ryan glanced up at her, his gaze assessing. "The scale looks precise and once we're outside, it will be easy for them to visualize exactly what you're proposing."

Charlie nodded and clapped her hands together. "They are fantastic, and I'm thrilled we found you last minute--it has to be a twist of fate that brought you to us."

Lucy's stomach tightened. Twist of fate indeed. From her peripheral vision, she caught the flare of Cam's nostrils, a movement he'd never been able to prevent when he was feeling stressed.

But where her emotions were ping-ponging around her chest, just like they had when she'd first met Cam all those years ago, Cam was unreadable. Was he truly unaffected by seeing her again? Or better at hiding his feelings than he used to be?

"Well, like we discussed last week, I feel my experience freelancing and handling all sorts of weddings really is the perfect background to build Cypress Coast Ranch into the peninsula's luxury wedding destination of choice. And the bonus is being able to reconnect with people from back in the day. I'm confident we'll seal this deal." Lucy beamed at Charlie and injected self-assurance into her voice.

"Like Charlie said, I think you're perfect for this role. Right, Cam?" Ryan said, his gaze flicking to his buddy.

Cam shrugged. "As long as I don't have to meet any more of the wedding people after today's meeting, it's all good." He glanced down at his large stainless-steel diver's watch. "We've got nine minutes before they arrive. Anything else to review?"

Ryan's brows drew together. "Cam, we've discussed this. When you manage a hotel, you've got to do whatever is necessary. With the level of competition in Monterey, we'll have to work our butts off to make this hotel a top contender Monterey wedding destination. You can't pick and choose what you do."

"I thought we hired a wedding planner so I could focus on opening and running the hotel." Cam's eyes narrowed.

"Dude, weddings will be vital to the success of this hotel. In the Army you knew how to do everyone's jobs, even though you were their boss. Think of it the same way. Some days you're commanding from the office and some days you're hanging garlands off a wedding arch." Ryan shrugged a shoulder.

Cam's jaw tightened. "Leading soldiers into battle and picking out flower schemes are the same––got it."

Charlie waved a hand and turned to Cam. "Think of it more like you're always ready and willing to assist anyone who needs it twenty-four/seven. That's how hospitality works––we're all in this together. Of course, your primary focus is on running the hotel smoothly. That includes honing our competitive strategy for creating Cypress Coast Ranch's reputation."

Cam squared his shoulders. "I was a Major in the Army. If you don't think I can handle it, tell me now."

Ryan sighed. "Of course you can handle it. No need to be so defensive."

"Fine." Cam gazed down at the scarred wooden conference table.

Maybe Cam hated weddings. Maybe it wasn't personal. But his behavior today revealed he didn't see their working together as destiny. More like an unwelcome necessity.

Lucy ran her tongue around her teeth. "I'm ready to manage the meeting and take the lead, since that's my role. We'll field the Harringtons' questions as they come. I suspect they will have ones specifically for each of you, so I'll defer those. Does that work for everyone?"

Cam lifted his gaze, respect in his eyes. "Great. I like the confidence."

Lucy shrugged a shoulder. So, he was paying attention. Had he realized she was a successful, experienced woman, not the wide-eyed college girl he'd left behind? Had he thought about her at all?

All those years ago, when their eyes locked outside the wide-open doors of East Bridge High School, lightning had speared through both their hearts. By the end of her first day of school Freshman year, she and Cameron Taylor had fallen head over heels in love. They'd been inseparable for six years.

Today, instead of passion and adoration in his eyes, his crystalline gaze held only professional respect.

Today, seeing him again, sparks danced up her spine and nerves flickered in her belly.

Sure, her physical reaction to seeing him again after so many years was only natural, right? Everyone was sentimental over their first love. Once the shock of seeing his big blond gorgeous self again wore off, she'd be perfectly fine.

She'd built her career in part by always maintaining her polished demeanor under any circumstances and today was no different. Lucy smoothed back a strand of hair and shook herself back to the present. Of course, they could forge a straightforward working relationship.

Fate may have thrown them back together, but today was all about cementing her role at Cypress Coast Ranch, not analyzing the startling emotional kick at finally seeing Cam again.

CHAPTER 2

ameron managed to keep his shit together. Barely. Sitting through this meeting with Lucy was more torturous than rehabbing his leg with his sadistic physical therapist. Twist of fate? More like payback time for every sin he'd ever committed.

Seeing her again was like a punch to the kidney--his fingers still burned from the featherlight brush against hers in the doorway. His visceral reaction had shocked him. Not that he'd allowed himself to brood over their unexpected reunion. Much.

When he'd first met Lucy at East Bridge High, she'd looked sweet and innocent with her enormous chocolate brown eyes and rosy cheeks. Lucy at twenty years old was beautiful but Lucy as a woman in full bloom? Devastating.

She'd cut her shiny sable hair so it skimmed her delicate shoulders and framed her oval face. His hands had itched to touch it and see if it was as silky as he remembered. She still favored bright colors, as evidenced by the cherry-red dress she wore. And she just glowed, so perhaps his prior fears about her health had been exaggerated.

When he'd set her free so she wouldn't have to worry whether he'd come home between tours or get injured--because that had gone according to plan--he figured she would have met someone new. Why wasn't she married? And why did the absence of a ring on her left hand matter to him--it wasn't like he was cut out for a happily ever after. His hands gripped his thighs under the table.

The enormous wood doors burst open, rousting him from his ruminations. Thank god.

Lucy rose and gracefully turned toward the stampeding stilettos invading his conference room. He gritted his teeth and resisted the urge to bolt and avoid the next hour of what was sure to be hell. Why had he believed running a hotel would be a cake walk after a dozen years as a military leader?

"Good morning, Victoria, Mrs. Harrington." Lucy glided across the room to greet the two platinum blondes built like greyhounds and swathed in museum sized jewels.

Victoria, the bride-to-be, inclined her head, her artificially full lips curved up in a facsimile of a smile. "Lucy, it's so nice to meet you in person." Her voice was pure saccharine.

"Call me Pamela," the matriarch said with a sniff. "And we're on a very tight schedule so we'd like to get started with the presentation. I must confess I'm a bit put off by all the construction happening around the property. You're sure it will be completed by next June?"

Lucy didn't flinch. "We're opening this May, so you've got nothing to worry about. We've got an excellent crew who will ensure the resort is completed in plenty of time. And our CEO and VP of Sales and Marketing, who flew in to meet you today, are getting married here this May."

Cam admired Lucy's poise. Not that she hadn't been bubbly and confident the last time he saw her, but she'd been a college junior. Her positive energy and warmth remained but she'd channeled it into impressive knowledge and capability.

On cue, Ryan and Charlie rose. "Hello Pamela and Victoria, I'm Ryan Michaels, CEO of the Hotel Kings Group. Welcome to our newest hotel."

Charlie skirted around the edge of the table and gestured for the women to join them. "And I'm Charlie Ray. Please have a seat. Lucy's going to start us off with a brief overview before we show you where we'll create your dream wedding."

The women settled around the table in a cloud of pungent perfume and Cam blew out an exhale. What he wouldn't give to be out with the construction crew right now. Or even be chained to his desk, buried in spreadsheets––anywhere but in a wedding planning meeting.

But damn it, this was his new assignment, and he never did anything half-assed. "Welcome to Cypress Coast Ranch, I'm Cam Taylor and I'm in charge of the hotel. We're looking forward to the opportunity to work with you."

Lucy clasped her hands together. "Wonderful. As Charlie said, we'll be out of here in just a few minutes, but let's watch a few slides before we tour the property. We'll have plenty of time for questions when we return."

Victoria yawned without bothering to cover her mouth. "Like my mother said, we're very busy. I'm either going to love it or I'm not. I don't see why we have to sit through some boring presentation."

"Stop it, Victoria. I made a point to ask Lucy for an overview first, so pay attention." Pamela's glacial tone could transform the Pacific into the world's largest ice-skating rink.

Lucy didn't miss a beat. She tucked a strand of hair behind her ear and beamed at Victoria. "I hear you. I promise I'll be fast because the grounds are absolutely one of a kind. Since some areas are under construction it's vital to see the completed plans so you can picture your perfect day."

Cam checked his watch and prayed Lucy stayed with the five-minute promise because he couldn't tear his eyes off of her. It was obvious she loved what she did and was damn good at it, her pitch clear and enthusiastic. Even though the exposition on theme colors and pergolas may as well have been in Latin for all he could understand.

He glanced over at Ryan and Charlie, who watched Lucy with rapt attention. So, he wasn't the only one pulled in by his ex-girlfriend's magnetism. Even the rude Harrington bride-to-be seemed to be listening. At least she'd put her phone face-down on the table.

An alarm dinged and Lucy raised her hand. "As promised, five minutes. So, let's head outside and I'll address your questions while we explore the grounds."

Ryan rose. "Ladies, if you'll excuse me, I've got a flight to catch. I want to assure you as head of Hotel Kings, we'll do whatever it takes to ensure your expectations are exceeded here. I'll leave you in these capable hands."

Cam slowly stood. He'd known Ryan since the first day of college at San Diego State University, where they'd started ROTC together, along with Jack and Lucas, their other partners. Ryan had come a long way––the guy was every inch the sophisticated CEO and hotel executive. After his time with the Army Reserve, Ryan had dedicated his entire career to living, breathing, and consuming the hotel industry. It showed.

"Thank you for coming. We'll see how it goes." Mrs. Harrington wasn't giving away much with her comment.

Victoria rose. "Yeah, thanks. Okay, let's see this place. At least the sun is out. I'm concerned about the fog and wind here. I need sunshine for my day."

Of course she did. Ryan caught Cam's eye. Pity the poor

guy who was marrying this chick. Nothing would make her happy.

Lucy chuckled and beamed at Victoria. "Oh, didn't I mention that's part of the package? Guaranteed sunshine?"

The woman's pinched face softened. "Well, in that case…"

Lucy was sunshine personified, and her potent warmth could even charm this woman. Just like she was thawing his determination to keep her at arm's length. Which was a path to disaster. He needed to ensure Lucy felt comfortable working for him and that meant keeping their relationship strictly business.

Cam waited until the group exited the conference room before following. Because of the incredible rehabilitation therapy he'd received in San Antonio after returning to the States, most days he had no limp. Some days he could run ten miles, just like he had in the Army. Some days, he'd use a cane.

Did Lucy know that his left lower leg had been blown to bits? Why would she?

Now that they'd be working together, he wouldn't be able to avoid telling her. He wouldn't be able to avoid *her*. His leg twinged and a shot of phantom pain ran down to his non-existent foot. Damn it--how was he going to work with her every day and keep his focus solely on running the hotel?

Charlie paused and waited for him. "You're coming with us, right? We need you to explain some of the finer points of the design and how the final resort will look."

"Just pulling up the rear and it looks like Lucy's got it under control," he said. Staying back in the safe zone.

Lucy was flanked by the Harrington women, several feet ahead of them.

Charlie tilted her head, her eyes narrowed. "Lucy's pretty incredible. You okay?"

"I'm fine. But I'd rather stay in the background on this

one. You guys call me in when I'm needed." Damn, she was shrewd. They'd become friends when she'd joined the company and he respected and liked Charlie. But he didn't talk about feelings. Just ask his assigned military psychologist or the guys trying to get him to group therapy.

Charlie smirked. "Like a pinch hitter?"

His lips twitched. "Yeah, basically. I know nothing about weddings and those women are a little scary."

"Talk about trial by fire. But weddings are key to this hotel's success, so you'll have to learn. Victoria Harrington is incredibly influential and if she loves it here, her millions of followers will flock to Cypress Coast Ranch. All weddings, all the time."

"We're already mostly booked out for a year without me being involved. Don't worry, I will make this hotel as successful as the others. And like you said, this is Lucy's arena." He would prove to everyone he could pull his weight.

Charlie rolled her eyes. "Famous last words." She stopped and laid one hand on his shoulder. "I'm not going to ask you about Lucy today but at some point, I'd really like to hear the story. I wasn't around back in the day, but Ryan said you two were serious."

Something tightened in Cam's chest. "It's ancient history. I'm sure you had a high school or college sweetheart. None of my business."

Charlie raised her dark brows. "Because my high school dating history has nothing to do with my current job. You and Lucy are going to be together a lot now and you're both single so…"

"Charlie. We are not having this discussion. Got it?" The last thing he needed was to be reminded Lucy was single.

"Okay, okay. But if--"

He held up one hand. "No."

"Cameron? Can you come up here and help explain these

plans for the glass-walled ballroom to Victoria and Pamela? We need your architectural knowledge," Lucy called over her shoulder.

"Of course." Happy to end Charlie's probing, he caught up with the other women. His architectural knowledge was basically non-existent, but he could parrot some of the information he'd gleaned from the actual building team.

And damn if the crisp January breeze didn't carry Lucy's citrus scent directly to him. His breath lodged in his throat. She still smelled like lemon and something sweet--like a lemon bar or lemon meringue pie. He'd always loved burying his face in her soft, glossy hair and drinking in her sweet yet tart scent. He was in big trouble.

"I've got a printout of the plans for the space, but you may be able to clarify the scale a little better." Lucy didn't appear affected by his proximity--she was pure business, like he needed to be.

She handed him the large, laminated document, her slender fingers brushing his, sending a shot of energy down his spine. Again.

He focused on the drawing. "I know right now this ballroom is just a shell because we gutted it, but it's going to be the main indoor space for weddings and receptions. We've reconfigured it so the entire West facing wall is a glass garage-style door that can be open or closed depending on the weather."

"If we choose the beach location and the weather is terrible, we can move in here? Will the staff be able to accommodate that kind of last-minute move?" Victoria wrinkled her nose.

He glanced at Lucy, who gave a quick nod and answered, "Of course. Unlike other venues, we will only have one wedding per day. You'll have the property to yourselves so if the Monterey weather doesn't cooperate, we've got Plan B."

Pamela's beady eyes narrowed and she placed her hands on her hips. "I do like that exclusivity. But Plan B cannot just be to move the outdoor set up indoors. We'd need two separate sets of plans drawn up and approved."

Lucy's smile didn't waver. "Absolutely. We'll ensure that Victoria's vision is implemented either way."

Victoria sniffed and checked her phone. "That sounds like a lot of work on your end. Most venues wouldn't be willing to plan two different ceremonies and receptions."

"We aren't most venues. Your colors and your flowers and your linens will be the same, right? I've prepared a few sketches of layouts for the gardens, the beach, and for this room, which we can review together. You'll have approval of everything before your big day, don't worry."

Victoria looped one arm through Lucy's. "I like you. We've seen a lot of venues and spoken to countless wedding planners. But you seem real. If the outdoor locations are as spectacular as the views from this place, this might just be where I'm getting married. Right, Mother?"

The elder Harrington woman's eyebrows rose. "Well, I haven't seen you this enthusiastic so far. But don't forget we have one more venue visit tomorrow. It will all come down to the details and the fine print in the contract."

"But you see the vision here, don't you?" Victoria wheedled.

"Let's keep on with the tour. We'll see," Pamela said.

"Excellent. Let's walk out to the gardens first." Lucy walked ahead with Victoria, who hadn't released her arm.

Cam wondered if Lucy knew she was likely selling her soul for this wedding. But Lucy was in charge, and unless her character had changed dramatically, no way would she promise unless she knew she could deliver.

Charlie and Cam fell into step behind the women. "Let's see if we can discover where they're going tomorrow so we can factor the information into the proposal," Charlie whispered.

"Excellent strategy. I'm sure Lucy will find out." A strong leader knew how to stay in the background when one of his people was winning. Lucy was obviously at the top of her game.

One of the reasons he'd broken up with Lucy before he went into the military was because he'd never wanted to hold her back. Would she have turned into such a powerhouse if she'd stayed with him and embraced the military wife life-style? Like him, maybe she thrived on dedicating everything to her career. He'd done the right thing.

So, what was with the hollow feeling in his chest?

CHAPTER 3

*L*ucy braced her hands on the edge of the conference table and blew out an exhausted exhale. Over the last decade, she'd methodically ascended the wedding planner ladder and today's meeting was the pinnacle. The last few hours had felt like scaling up the sheer granite face of Half-Dome, one of Yosemite's highest peaks. Not that she'd ever had the desire to hike the famous rock, but she'd observed the daredevil climbers from the safety and beauty of the valley floor.

The Harringtons had been as difficult as she'd anticipated but being "on" for three hours straight was no joke. Three long hours. Their scheduled ninety minutes had been blasted through by endless questions, Pamela Harrington's demands they sketch out the exact placement for chairs, the wedding gazebo, and each detail. The mother and daughter duo had tested Lucy's knowledge and patience, but her gut assured her she'd hooked them.

Joy filled her and she grinned at the bluebird day outside the clear windowpanes. Her first booking as the official Wedding and Events Planner of Cypress Coast Ranch would be one of the most publicized weddings of the year. Heck, of the decade, if Victoria had her way.

"Do we have a deal?" Cam's husky voice interrupted her inner celebration.

He stood framed in the doorway, his hands in the pockets of his casual dark slacks, his face unreadable.

She straightened to her full height of 5 foot 6, which included her four-inch stilettos. Even so, Cam practically loomed over her at just over six feet.

Her pulse kicked up, but she kept her voice level. "Not yet but we will. Mrs. Harrington asked for a detailed proposal, with pricing, adding in all the information we covered today. I'll have it to her by close of business."

"You sound confident." His expression remained neutral.

She nodded. "I am. I've been doing this for years and I've worked with clients just like the Harringtons. They loved it and I'm not worried about the site they are visiting tomorrow."

"You were great. I was impressed how you handled them both. I don't know how you stayed so patient." His voice was gruff.

"Thanks." Okay this was a conversation between two acquaintances––awkward. She shrugged. "It's what I do."

He quirked a blond brow. "Handle difficult people?"

She ran her tongue around her teeth. "Well, I handled you for years, right?"

He squeezed his eyes shut for a moment and his lips quirked. "I walked right into that one, didn't I?"

"Pretty much." She smirked and tucked a lock of hair behind her ear.

He advanced a few steps into the room, his eyes narrowed. "How are you, Lucy?"

"You mean now or in general? Or did you want a year-by-year account from the last time we saw each other?" And so much for maintaining a professional distance. Now he was checking in on her?

He sucked in a sharp inhale. "Lucy, I––"

Annoyance flared and she crossed her arms across her chest. "I just want to be clear. Because you made it crystal clear thirteen years ago that you were walking out of my life for good. And by some wild coincidence, here *we* are. I've got a lot of work to do to secure this wedding. So, we don't have time today for the full reunion. But I'm just fine, thanks for asking."

His nostrils flared. "Look, I did what I thought was best for you––"

A haze of red obscured her gaze. "What you thought was best for me? Your ego hasn't changed, I see. Relationships are a two-way street and you never even asked me what I wanted. You just decided I was too damn fragile or something to handle long-distance or stress. After everything I've been through in my life, that's a joke."

He massaged the back of his neck. "I know you're not fragile. Damn it, I was twenty-two and you were barely twenty. You had our whole life planned out for us."

"Sure, we were young, but I knew what I wanted." She grabbed her briefcase––time to retreat. "I need to draft the contract, so I'm heading out."

"It wasn't like I didn't know how I felt, Lucy, I was just trying to be practical. Realistic. You know I was commissioned as an officer, that I'd be sent overseas. It's a difficult life." His brows drew together.

Her fingers dug into the leather handle, and she struggled to tamp down the emotions bubbling up in her throat. "Again, you never gave me the choice. And whether life is easy or difficult is all a matter of perspective. Like I said, I need to finish this proposal by tonight. If you'll excuse me." She marched past him to the doorway.

He stepped back and allowed her to pass without another word, but his eyes burned into her as she maintained a steady pace away from him. Every nerve ending in her body urged her to break into a run, but she refused to succumb. She'd look casual and cool if it killed her. No way would she allow him to see the trembling of her limbs or the beads of perspiration on her forehead.

Once she'd escaped to the parking lot, she wrenched open the door to her red Subaru Forester, clambered inside, and slammed the door. Anger and hurt battled for the top spot inside her and she hugged her arms around her middle. Ever since the night he'd broken her heart, she'd dreamt and daydreamt of what she would say to him if she ever saw him again. *If* being a major factor.

She glanced toward the main building's entrance, but Cam hadn't followed her. Thank goodness. She was thirty seconds from a full-on meltdown and he couldn't witness it. His last memory of her had been her sobbing and collapsing, shattered, onto the earth.

Today, she'd replaced that image with uber-professional badass and that's how he would see her. Strong. Capable. Independent. Heart-whole.

Lucy fired up the ignition and breathed steadily through her nose. In for four. Out for four. Soothing and calming for her nervous system. As she pulled out of the expansive parking lot and pointed her car toward home, the tears started to fall. Not gut-wrenching sobs but pure gushing waterfalls of pain pouring from her eyes. She didn't bother to wipe her drenched cheeks.

The memories flashed through her. That night, she'd tingled in anticipation at his choice to spend the evening at their favorite park, where they'd whiled away countless hours over the years. She'd worn her favorite navy and scarlet striped dress and spent hours on her hair and make-up, anticipating a proposal and some engagement photos.

That terrible night, she'd been confident he would propose. That even though she had two years of college to finish, they'd continue long-distance until she could join him wherever he was stationed. Not so much. Instead, he told her it was over and to move on with her life without him. Shock had stolen her words and she'd never seen him again until today. Never expressed how she'd felt.

Of course, after the fact, she had written him letter after letter, saying all the things she wished she had said when he blindsided her. But she'd never mailed them. What was the point? Her pride wouldn't allow her to beg him to reconsider. And when Cam made up his mind, he didn't change it.

Seeing Cam again had dredged up memories and feelings she'd assumed would remain dormant. Even though their relationship had ended thirteen years ago, she certainly hadn't gotten proper closure. And his comments today about doing what was best and realistic for both of them? With no discussion?

No. No. No.

Deep in her heart, she'd believed if they were meant to be, he would realize he'd made a mistake, return to her with some grand gesture worthy of a romance novel, and beg for a second chance. Not so much.

Instead, fate had tossed them back together. And although she couldn't deny her attraction to him, the fact remained he was her boss and they needed to navigate this new curve in the road. Besides, there was no way she could ever trust him with her heart again.

For the next few miles along quiet roads to her cozy renovated cottage just off Prescott, she simply cried. Once she stepped into her place, the tears would stop. Tonight, she would compartmentalize all of it until she'd hit send on the Harrington proposal.

She could compartmentalize with the best of them. One of her therapists when she'd been a child had given her an incredible exercise that stuck with her today. If it works when you're on death's door at age eight, it certainly worked as a grown woman. The valuable lesson she'd learned was that for any challenge, whether it be illness or heartbreak, it can easily take over your entire life if you let it. It's easy to identify with the pain and tumble into the world of being just a victim.

She'd learned she could decide to give the challenge a certain amount of time, but then cut it off. Like changing the TV channel. When she was little, she'd say, "Cancer can have part of my time, but not all of my time. I will not be defined by it."

And after Cam left her, she'd substituted the word heartbreak for cancer. She'd learned to visualize paradise and for her that had been a hammock on a deserted white sand beach, with a beloved book, and a frozen drink. A Slurpee had become a pina colada, but the rest remained the same to this day. After a while, she was able to relegate her first love to the past.

Lucy sat taller in her seat when her cottage came into view. Once she entered the small adjoining garage, no more reminiscing. Her entire focus would remain on the incredible opportunity in front of her until she was satisfied. Once she finished the proposal, she could contemplate the convoluted mix of emotions flowing through her.

She parked, killed the engine, and exited the car. When Lucy glanced up at the charming 1940s Spanish style house, her muscles softened. There was something magical about the place that suited her perfectly. It was tiny with one bedroom and an alcove that served as her den where she could feel separate from the rest of the living space and focus on work. Granted, the closet only held about four outfits and a pair of shoes, but that's what the gorgeous antique wardrobe she'd found at an estate sale was for.

She unlocked the cobalt blue front door and stepped into the cozy living room, complete with a wood-burning fireplace framed by built-in bookshelves. A large crimson rug covered the center of the space, contrasting against the deep oak hardwood floors. The original plaster walls were filled with watercolor paintings that reflected the nearby Pacific and cypress trees. Northern California's raw wild beauty had always tugged at her heart.

Moving from Santa Cruz to Monterey two years ago with her best friend Sue had been a great choice. They'd met in college and instantly bonded during their excruciatingly mind-numbing Economics class. Now they were not just friends but neighbors. After she sent the winning proposal to the Harringtons and cc'd Charlie and Cam, she would pour an enormous glass of chardonnay and call Sue to dissect the situation.

Lucy crossed to the modest kitchen with its black and white patterned tile floor and cheerful white walls. Although her wine fridge beckoned, she ignored the call of the grapes and squeezed fresh lemon into a glass of sparkling water.

Work first.

Wine and whine later.

Time to get her professional life secured because her personal life looked precarious, at least for a while. She carried her drink to her vintage roll-top desk, unpacked her laptop, and started to type. This time next week she'd celebrate kicking off her fabulous new job by landing the wedding of the year.

THE CLASSIC GRAY Monterey afternoon suited Cam's mood perfectly. He slowed to a walk, the breeze off the water chilling his skin through his thin weather-tech running clothes. Today was one of those days the sparks of phantom pain plagued him. He'd powered through the five miles on the path around the bay anyway. After spending the day with Lucy, he'd needed to wrestle with the major problem seeing her again presented.

He'd assumed it would be simple to keep their relationship strictly business. Had assumed the attraction between them was a thing of the past. Damned if he hadn't been blindsided by desire for her. Adjusting to working in the civilian world for the first time wasn't easy. Pitching in the 5-foot-2 wrench into what seemed like a straightforward operation rendered the future more challenging.

Cam surveyed his pristine house as he strode to the master bathroom, peeled off his tank top and nylon running pants, and tossed them in the clothes hamper inside his walk-in closet. His clothes hung in precise rows, evenly spaced, and yeah, even color-coded. Maybe he was anal, but since he had extra steps most people didn't, like attaching and removing his prosthetic, saving time was critical.

He sat on the small wooden bench outside his enormous custom shower. In addition to the existing guard rail on the gray tiled shower wall, Cam had bought a new shower chair, which sat beneath the mounted hand-held shower head. Although his core strength and balance were excellent, no need to screw around and play a hero. He'd done that in Afghanistan and he'd lost one of his men and his left leg for his efforts.

No need to break a hip falling in the shower.

Damn, he never thought he'd think about injuring himself in the shower at age 35.

But here he was. He unfastened his state-of-the-art below

the knee limb, slid off the compression sock, and set them in their stand. He massaged his residual limb, like his therapist in San Antonio had taught him. The earlier stabbing pains he'd experienced had mercifully subsided and now he just had some low-intensity soreness like he usually did after an intense run.

From here, it was a shift to the shower chair using one of the rails. He flipped on the shower to scorching hot and tilted his head back and sighed as the pounding water rained down on him. Even though the shower chair was a pain in the ass, he couldn't deny it felt pretty decadent. He wasn't a bath guy--gross to sit in your own dirty water--but reclining while showering worked.

What would Lucy think? She'd always loved fooling around in the shower and somehow his geriatric set up wasn't exactly conducive to steamy shower sex. His eyes flew open, and his entire body leapt to attention. What the hell was he doing thinking about Lucy, naked, slick, and slippery in the shower?

Seeing her today-- how she'd grown from girl to badass woman--had been a right-cross to his jaw. She'd been magnificent and had blown away not just the Harringtons, Ryan and Charlie, but him too.

Memories of their six years together came flooding back, even the ones he'd only allowed himself on some of the dark lonely nights abroad. He exhaled an unsteady breath.

Damn it, he'd only questioned two major decisions in his life. Usually, he simply knew what to do--his instincts were part of what made him such a great leader. Well, until the end. Checking on his patrol in the streets of the small village, even when he should have stayed back, had been a mistake that essentially ended his career.

And now he realized maybe he'd screwed up when he broke up with Lucy.

Could the last decade have worked between them? Would he have had enough energy to give her the attention she deserved while he served on four long tours of duty in Afghanistan and Iraq? Would she have progressed as far with her career if she'd been forced to move around with him?

Lucy had every right to be pissed at him and whether he liked it or not, they would have to revisit their past to move forward. Based on her performance today, regardless of whether they got the Harrington wedding, she was with Hotel Kings to stay.

He flipped off the shower, grabbed a fluffy navy towel, and scrubbed the moisture off his face. If he approached the situation with Lucy like any other career mission, he knew what to do. It was up to him to ensure that Lucy felt comfortable on the job. Once the initial shock of seeing each other again wore off, they would be able to work together like any other colleagues.

He had this assignment completely under control.

CHAPTER 4

*L*ucy pushed away from her desk, paced to the kitchen, and yanked open the heavy stainless-steel refrigerator door. For the past hour, her stomach had been grumbling. She contemplated the pathetic contents––her choices were raspberries with a risky expiration date or chocolate swirl pudding. Pudding reminded her of finishing treatment days when she was a kid––a symbol of comfort. At least she'd refrained from buying the cool whip. Maybe if she put the fruit into the pudding, it would count as a proper meal. Fruit group, plus dairy and protein.

Rationalization complete, she peeled off the foil lid and licked off the excess pudding that remained. No need to waste it, right? She plucked out the six raspberries that had not succumbed to a mossy covering and dropped them on top. She scooped up the biggest spoonful possible and savored the explosion of flavors on her tongue. Then she snorted, imagining the Harringtons' face if she suggested pudding as a wedding dessert instead of a mousse or crème pot.

She returned to her desk and stared at the proposal she'd

printed out again--as if the answers she needed would magically materialize. If only. Part of the problem of coming into the job at the last minute--she still hadn't completed a full tour of Cypress Coast Ranch herself.

She scraped the bottom of the plastic pudding cup--these servings were for little kids, not hungry adults--and set down the container.

She'd promised to send the proposal to Victoria and Pamela by 8 p.m., but she lacked the full picture, like the specs and details for some of the outdoor spaces. If her calculations were off by one guest chair or two millimeters of aisle space, it would be an epic disaster.

No alternative existed except to call Cam. Unless he knew some of these details off the top of his head, they'd need to rendezvous at the hotel. Without the protection of other people around them. She squeezed her eyes closed.

Today had already been a long day and her defenses weren't what they'd been eight hours ago. But what choice did she have? Business came first.

If she failed to win this bid, who knew if they'd even keep her on at the hotel? With a heavy sigh, she picked up her phone and scrolled through her contacts until she reached Cam's number. Her heart pinched when she reached his name. Who would've thought she'd ever have him listed in her phone again?

The phone rang once, twice, three times...would he send her to voicemail? On the fifth ring, he answered, sounding slightly breathless. "Lucy?"

"Did I catch you at a bad time?" And why did his low growly voice still kickstart her pulse?

"No, just coming out of the shower. Everything okay?"

A vision of his lean chiseled frame flashed before her eyes. *Down girl.* "I'm sorry to bother you, but I can't finish the

Harrington proposal without a few more property details. Do you have some time?"

The line went silent for a few moments. "Yeah, of course. What do you need to know?"

"How well do you know the dimensions of the gardens, the beach, and the ballroom? Mrs. Harrington requires we provide the exact number of chairs that could fit into each area, with specific measurements, down to the minute detail. I could guesstimate it from the perimeter numbers I have but I have a feeling that woman would come out with a tape measurer and double check."

Cam chuckled. "That sounds about right. Well, off the top of my head, the answer is no. Can you meet me over there in fifteen? The sun will be setting in about half an hour, so we need to be quick."

"Of course. Shall I meet you in the gardens?" Her shoulders relaxed.

"Perfect. We'll get the dimensions as close as possible. Let me throw on some clothes and hop in the car."

She sucked in a sharp inhale. Was he alluding to getting naked on purpose, or was he that oblivious? "Great. See you there."

Lucy glanced down at her ancient SFSU sweatshirt and yoga leggings. No time to change and really, did it matter? The job was the priority, not wearing a cute outfit to make Cam regret dumping her. Besides, she'd already worn her favorite dress and given the presentation of her life earlier today.

She hurried to the bathroom to brush her teeth and comb her hair. She could slick on some lip gloss in the car. They needed to learn to work together without personal feelings interfering, but a little lip gloss never hurt.

Right?

~

Lucy stepped out of her car just as Cam parked his vintage Jeep next to her. Well, that was a first--she'd actually beat Mr. Punctual. Back in the day, Cam ran on military time even before ROTC and never needed a clock. Whereas she'd never been a morning person and always needed an alarm. He stepped out of his car, his short wheat-colored hair damp and a hint of scruff covering his chiseled jawline.

Her heart stuttered--she was in major trouble. Plenty of time after she'd sent off the proposal to ponder how much his proximity impacted her. She hurried toward him. "Ready?"

He held up an industrial chrome tape measure. "If you've got the notebook to record it, I can measure it."

She hugged her pink puffy coat tight and adjusted her thick scarf around her neck. The temperature had plummeted since their first tour of the property. Once the sun started to set in Northern California, especially near the water, it got cold quick. "Should we go out to the private beach first?"

He nodded and they crossed the large parking lot together. "Yeah, that way we can take advantage of the remaining sunlight. We've got some artificial lights in the gardens. You've got the external dimensions, right?" He tilted his head toward her, one brow raised.

"Yeah, but I really need to see how far out we can go on the perimeters and such. The sketches have to be more accurate than what I put together before." Nothing less than perfection for the Harringtons.

"No problem."

And Mr. Quiet was back. Not that Cam had ever been a talkative guy, but he could get into deep discussions when it suited him. When he was comfortable. Back in college, they'd spent hours on the phone and never run out of words. His deep, raspy voice saying "I love you" had been the last thing she'd hear every night before dropping off to sleep. When they'd been in love.

They crested the grassy hill to the small bluff above the resort's private beach, which was surrounded by a low, split-rail fence. Lucy's breath caught in her throat and the breeze stung her cheeks, the salt mist carrying up from where the waves pounded into the pale sand beach.

The twilight sky was filled with violet and rose streaks, and the sun hung low, ready to slide beneath the tumbling white-capped gray surf. Fingers of fog hung in the brisk early evening air. "Wow. It never gets old, does it?" Lucy gazed up at Cam, who was staring out at the horizon.

He shook his head. "No. But we need to hurry. What numbers do you need?"

"I need to have aisle space around the outside to mark the end of the rows and the walkway for everyone to make their way out here. Also, I'm assuming she'll want an extra wide aisle up to the gazebo where they'll say their vows. And she's got twelve bridesmaids and groomsmen, so it has to all fit and not look crowded."

His chiseled jaw went slack. "Twelve bridesmaids? Are you kidding me? I thought she was an only child?"

Lucy laughed. "She is. These are all friends, believe it or not. This is why our policy of only one wedding per day is excellent and the Harringtons renting out the entire resort is so vital."

His eyes widened. "I don't know how you handle these kinds of demands all the time."

She gave a half-shrug. "I love what I do. Creating weddings that are the perfect expression for each individual couple makes me happy. Believe me, most of the couples I work with are wonderful and it doesn't feel like work. But even difficult people deserve a beautiful wedding, right?"

"I don't know. It seems like people waste a ton of money that they could use on a down-payment on a house or a killer trip." He shook his head again.

She stiffened. "A waste? You're running a hotel now that's going to be a major wedding venue and you probably want to keep that opinion to yourself." *Had he always been this annoying?*

His ice-blue eyes caught hers. "It's just you and me right now. Plus, like I said earlier, I don't plan on having much interaction with the day to day of it."

She threw back her head and laughed. "Sorry Cam, you're in the wedding business now. Oh, the irony."

His nostrils flared. "The irony?"

"Everyone knows you're terrified of commitment so it's pretty funny if you consider it. But let's get those dimensions, okay?" *And so much for keeping it professional and compartmentalizing.* Now that she was with him, all the retorts and regrets of the last thirteen years were bubbling out.

"I'm not terrified of commitment." He lifted his square chin.

"Whatever you say." She shivered when another artic gust bit through her clothes. "It's freezing out here so can we get this done?"

His lips pressed into a tight line. "Fine. Let's start at the south edge." Without waiting for her, he turned and marched toward the opposite end of the sandy cove.

He was favoring his left leg. Joy, who had passed the job opportunity along to her, had shared that Cam had resigned his commission early after an injury in Afghanistan. Although Lucy was highly curious, she hadn't wanted to pry, especially when they were on shaky ground. She would ask

Cam when the time was right. Which most definitely was not right now.

She trudged toward him on the shifting sand. She'd focus on numbers for the proposal and bolt out of there as soon as she could. Apparently, her emotions were getting the better of her and she couldn't stem the sarcasm or ignore the past hurt. The clock was ticking, and tonight wasn't the time for a heart-to-heart.

For all she knew, he'd keep her at arm-distance forever. His walls were high, and did she even want to go there? Not now, anyway. She sighed and continued to push her emotions to the back chamber of her heart.

The sun continued its inexorable descent beneath the horizon but there wasn't time to savor it. Despite her puffy jacket, she was already chilled through. For the next fifteen minutes, Cam measured and called out numbers and she logged them with freezing fingers. They could have been complete strangers completing tasks. What a contrast to their six-year intimate relationship.

After surviving the tension on the beach, they moved to the gardens. Luckily, the gorgeous grounds had man-made edges, unlike the beach, which maintained its natural borders. Cam flipped on some outdoor lights that flooded the area. The sky had morphed from pale lavender and pink to a deep violet streaked with charcoal clouds and shadows settled around the fenced-in area just outside the ballroom doors.

Methodically, she continued recording the figures he called out and double-checked she had all the information she'd need to create the proposed seating arrangements. No chit-chat, no talking at all. She softened her jaw, not wanting to grind her molars into dust. Irritation stiffened her spine––couldn't he at least try to be friendly? Had he always been so pig-headed and mono-syllabic? And why did she care? They were co-workers now and nothing more.

Once they finished, they entered the ballroom. Lucy resisted the urge to step out of business mode.

She surveyed the vast open space. "Well, this is easier. If we have to move indoors, the layout is going to be completely different than if we're on the beach or in the gardens. But it should still work."

"Yeah, the walls make it simple. Do you already have all these dimensions?" Cam had crossed to the opposite corner of the ballroom, yet the intensity of his presence filled the room. He quirked a brow, his expression neutral.

She drew in a steadying breath. "I have enough to finish the proposal, probably just in the nick of time. But I think we need to resolve the past, so everything isn't as awkward as it feels right now. When can we sit down and catch up?" Her exhale whooshed out.

His wary crystalline eyes met hers. "Is that what you want to do?"

For some reason, his answering her question with a question irritated her. "I don't know if want is the right word, but I think that given our history and the fact you're now my boss, it's probably a good idea, right?" How was this not obvious?

"You mean start fresh?" He shoved his hands into his pockets.

"I don't know what it looks like, Cam. But yeah, maybe that's it. I still need some closure and we need a clear path moving forward, okay?" Her gut tightened.

His eyebrows drew together. "I don't know if I can give you closure, but you're right, we need to put the past where it belongs. I want you to feel comfortable working here."

She swallowed the nerves fluttering in her throat. "Then, it makes sense to talk sooner than later—I'll text you in the morning. I need to head back and finish the proposal. Thanks for helping me out."

"Okay. And I'm here to help––it's my hotel."

And once again he was all business. Maybe that's how he was with everyone now––she'd just never been on the receiving end. Yeah, they needed to clear the air sooner than later. No way was she going to allow their past to jeopardize her new career.

Although now she'd seen Cam again, she wasn't sure how she'd be able to pull off that miracle.

CHAPTER 5

Cam parked his jeep at Seaside State Beach, where he'd agreed to meet Lucy for a walk along the Monterey Bay Coastal Recreation Trail. He grimaced and massaged the tight muscles of his left quadriceps, willing the familiar cramping to subside. Maybe he'd pushed himself too far on his runs this week--but he'd craved the endorphins. Every damn day when he put on or took off his prosthetic leg, he was reminded of his time overseas.

Damn it, when he'd resigned his commission and joined his best friends to create Hotel Kings, LLC, he'd resolved to begin a new life. A second chance, a new purpose after his lifelong dream career ended. But flashbacks and nightmares were his frequent companions and refused to allow him to forget all the soldiers who'd lost their lives or been injured carrying out his orders.

Time to tamp down on his survivor's guilt and deal with what was currently contributing to his sleepless nights--Lucy.

When she'd texted him asking to meet up, his first impulse was to dodge their conversation. But he was an adult, and it was his duty to guide them to level ground. Although, he wasn't sure how re-hashing the past would resolve anything between them. If he'd spent years convincing himself he'd done the right thing and still had doubts, how could he give her closure?

And what exactly was closure anyway? He glanced at his watch and stepped out of his SUV. No use procrastinating. He'd faced hell in Iraq and Afghanistan so he should be able to face his ex-girlfriend.

"Cam," Lucy's sweet voice called.

She strode toward him wearing a pair of violet running tights, a white puffer jacket, and a pom-pom topped yellow knit beanie. The hat was perfect for Monterey's winter weather and framed her heart-shaped face. Her high cheekbones were flushed pink, and her enormous dark eyes sparkled.

He raised a hand in greeting. Something unfamiliar tugged in his chest––how had he forgotten the power of her beauty? Her sweet bright personality glowed from the inside out.

She stopped when she reached him and tilted her head back to gaze into his eyes. "You ready to walk?" Without her stilettos, Lucy barely reached his shoulder. He used to joke he could put her in his pocket.

"Yeah, let's do this." They fell into step together and headed south on the wide path. Although the sun was out, the pastel blue sky was dotted with clouds and the wind off the Pacific was downright chilly. Neither of them spoke for a few minutes. Initiating talks about anything other than work wasn't his wheelhouse.

She huffed out a breath. "You're not going to make this easy, are you?"

He gazed down at her. "Easy? In what world is this talk easy? The past is the past––it was another lifetime and I'm not sure what to say but I want you to feel comfortable working with me. I think we should focus on moving forward."

"No." She shook her head, her eyes narrowed. "No way. The past is what shaped us both into who we are today. You can't pretend that our relationship and our break-up and the intervening years didn't happen. And there's no way to move forward without reconciling it."

He gritted his teeth. "We broke up thirteen years ago. We were kids. I'm sorry that I handled it the way I did. But I'm not sure what else to say after all this time."

Her full pink lips thinned. "An apology isn't enough. You owe me an explanation. You just made up your mind that you knew best and bailed on me after six years together. Your ability to switch off your emotions and walk away like I never mattered is something I would like to understand."

His throat clenched. "You mattered, Lucy. You've always mattered. That wasn't it." Sure, he'd decreed they had no future, but he'd never meant her to feel like he hadn't valued her.

She wrapped her arms around her slender waist and peered up from beneath the fringe of her thick black lashes. "It didn't feel that way. You just *told* me that you were leaving. No chance to discuss it. No time for us to sit down and really figure out what that meant. One minute, I thought we'd continue long-distance while I finished school--which had worked out really well for the first few years you were at San Diego State by the way--the next you're gone without a backward glance."

He tilted his head back and massaged the staccato beat starting in his temples. "Long distance in the same state and long distance while I'm leading troops in a war zone and you're attending English Lit class are not the same thing."

Her hands moved to her hips. "No kidding. Gee, I thought

it would be easy breezy. But I was willing to try. You didn't even want to try." Her voice wobbled.

He winced. Direct hit. "I was trying to do the best thing for you. Believe me, it was the hardest decision I've ever made."

She poked one mittened hand against his chest. "Best for me? You decided? You sound like my father."

He blanched and quickly looked away. He had a poker face, but Lucy had always been able to read him.

Her eyes flashed and she shoved him. "What? You're hiding something from me."

Damn it. "It doesn't matter. It was still the right decision. You didn't need to be worrying about whether I'd come back. You needed to create a life you loved, and you've done that. I would have held you back."

Her eyes narrowed and the rosy flush in her cheeks intensified to twin red flags. "Oh, you are so full of it. I loved you and nothing holds me back when I want something, you know that. But you made a face when I mentioned my dad. What does he have to do with this?"

His hands curled into fists inside his leather gloves. "Okay, your dad and I had a talk before I left for training. He said some things that made sense and maybe it influenced my decision to break things off and let us each start fresh."

"Ooooh." She growled. "I can only imagine. I just can't believe you bought it. For some reason, my father still sees me as a seven-year-old with cancer. Even now, he feels like he has to protect me and check in on me. Like he had anything to do with me getting sick. Or he could prevent me getting sick again. Not that he or you can control any of it."

"Well, he had a point. I mean, you're one of the strongest, most resilient people I know. And Lucy, you were so damn certain. But I needed to dedicate myself to the military. To see the world. To grow up." He shrugged. "I don't know. I was worried I wouldn't live up to this perfect vision you had for us. I had to give my all to the Army.

She sucked in a breath. "You're saying you felt trapped by me?"

He winced. "Damn it, Lucy, I'm not good at expressing myself. Not trapped but you were so certain you knew our future, and I needed to discover it for myself. And what if I'd been deployed and you'd gotten sick?"

"For all you know, maybe I did." Her brows rose.

His heart slammed against his ribs. "You didn't, did you?"

She waved one hand at him. "No. But no thanks to you. Did you and my father ever consider, even once in your 'oh, we'll protect delicate little Lucy' discussion that you breaking my heart might have weakened me so much the cancer returned?"

His throat went dry––she had a point. "No, we're idiots."

"Not that you checked in on me or anything, but I couldn't eat, I couldn't sleep, I barely made it through Fall semester after you bailed. You broke my heart." Her melted-chocolate eyes shone with the gleam of unshed tears and her words trailed off in a whisper.

He stopped and led them to the railing at the edge of the path. She kept her arms hugged around her waist. "Lucy, I never meant to hurt you. You were the love of my life, and you always came first. Part of me worried I wouldn't be able to give you the attention you deserved while I was building my career. Looking back now, I don't know if I could have been there for you the way you deserved. The Army was all-consuming."

She searched his gaze and he forced himself not to look away. To allow her to see his sincerity. "So, you needed to do it on your own and see how life unfolded? You were scared you'd screw it up at some point, is that it?"

He gave a half-shrug. "In retrospect, yeah. Afraid I'd

screw up one or the other. I didn't think I had it in me to be the best commander and be the best partner for you."

She turned and stared out at the white-capped surf pounding onto the beach. His fingers itched to reach out and smooth the silky dark strand of hair away from her cheek, but he curled his hand into a fist instead. The last thing she wanted right now was him to touch her.

He'd never expected to see her again. And now she was here, memories flooded in——Lucy's distinctive loud laugh that seemed too boisterous for her petite frame, her sweet kisses, her genuine compassion and care not just for him but for everyone she met. Hell, he'd never deserved her.

"Even though I disagree with your reasoning, I think you're more than capable of handling yourself on every level, I understand where you were coming from. I just wish you'd given us a chance. Sat down and talked about it with me. Maybe we could have left the door open."

"Left the door open?"

She turned and tilted her head up to meet his gaze. "If we'd talked about it and you'd shared what you were worried about, we didn't have to break up. We could have tried, seen what happened, heck, I don't know. You were so cold. Like we'd never been in love."

He swallowed the bitter taste rising in his throat. "I didn't know how else to do it. I had to stay focused on the end result."

"Well, it sucked. And you ruined me for other guys." Her eyes narrowed.

"What do you mean?" His gut tightened.

She bit her lip and studied the horizon again. "Let's just say once I finally recovered to the point where I actually went out with someone again, I had a tough time trusting."

"It's been a long time. You've had serious relationships,

right?" What man wouldn't fight to win Lucy's heart? Yeah, he'd screwed that one up.

She lowered her thick lashes, hiding her eyes. "Yeah, a few long-term ones. But in the end, they haven't worked out. What about you?"

He considered. "No, nothing beyond casual. I meant what I said about giving everything to the Army. I did four tours in Iraq and Afghanistan and work always came first."

"But tons of men and women in the military are married, have families. They make it work." A small crease formed between her winged eyebrows.

"Sure. But that wasn't for me." Like anyone could have compared to Lucy. Fun women who wanted to date, hook up when he was in town with no strings—that's who he'd settled for.

"Weren't you lonely?" Her eyes widened and her pink lips parted.

He shrugged. "I've always been good on my own." No need to admit that memories of her had haunted him on many a sleepless night in Iraq.

She shivered. "I'm getting cold standing here. Can we keep walking?"

"Yeah, you never get used to the way this wind bites through you." They turned and joined the rest of the pedestrians traversing the wide paved trail.

January wasn't a big month for tourists, so it was mostly locals out for a run or bike ride or walk this morning. Cyclists cruised along in their own lane. The rugged beauty of the coast was enticing enough for people to cope with the misty fog and the damp chill. The water was a deep indigo, the sand undisturbed, and the rocks and boulders emphasized the raw majesty of nature. It reminded him that it was good to be alive. Despite it all.

They walked in silence for a few minutes—maybe she'd

gotten the answers she needed. His gut was churning, and he forced himself to tuck away what she'd shared to analyze later. What kind of asshole was he?

"So, you dedicated yourself to the Army, but you resigned your commission early. I know you were injured but I don't know what happened. Will you tell me?" She brushed his forearm and even through her thick wool mitten and his down jacket, his system jolted.

Chemistry had never been an issue between them. Hell, they hadn't had any issues between them. He shook himself back. May as well tell her all of it now so they could move forward and start fresh. She'd understand how in the end he was right––she was better off without him.

He blew out a deep breath. "Me and a few of my guys were patrolling a small village. Hit a landmine."

She gasped and turned. "A landmine? Oh my god Cam, you're lucky to be alive. That's terrible."

"I lost one of my men and lost the lower half of my leg." A wave of nausea rolled through him, and he swallowed down the bile in his throat.

She stopped and looked down at his sweat pant covered leg. "I had no idea. And I'm so sorry you lost one of your guys."

His jaw tightened. "Thanks. Some days are better than others. I ran ten miles this morning so I'm sore but some days I use a cane. The prosthetic is state of the art, but it can be a real pain in the ass."

"Oh Cam." Before he knew what was happening, she stepped into him and wound her arms around his waist and laid her head against his chest. He stiffened, his arms useless by his side, his mind blank.

Lucy snuggled in closer. "I'm so sorry. Please hug me back."

Unable to resist, he banded his arms around her and

pulled her against him, accepting the comfort she offered. He dropped his cheek to rest on top of her head, the tickle of fluffy pom-pom soft against his skin. She held on tight, every ounce of her committed to sharing comfort in the way only she knew how.

Slowly, awareness of every inch of her compact little body plastered against him filtered through his senses. Through Herculean self-control, he managed to keep his hands in place and not stroke down her spine to clasp her ass and rock her into his burgeoning hard-on. *Danger.* He clasped her waist and started to set her away from him. No way could he be this close to her.

She glanced up at him, her chocolate brown eyes soft, her tempting lips parted.

Panic tickled his throat. "Lucy." His heart slammed against his ribs.

"Cam." Her pupils flared.

Fuck it. Slowly, he lowered his mouth and brushed his lips against her impossibly soft ones. She melted against him, deepening the kiss, stroking and swirling her tongue with his. He groaned at her delicious taste and skimmed his hands up to her jaw to hold her in place. His mind emptied and everything else faded into the background.

She pressed her hands against his chest. "It's freezing out here. Do you want to come over and have some coffee? I want to hear more about what happened. More about your time overseas." Her eyelids were heavy, her voice breathy.

He jolted back to reality. What were they doing? Where was his self-control? Time to retreat. "I've got to get over to the hotel. And I'd rather not talk about that period of time."

She didn't blink but she stepped back. "Okay. Thanks for discussing our break-up with me and thanks for the kiss. And for the record, you were wrong. I was certain we would have made it."

With that pronouncement, she turned and sauntered away, leaving him alone with the icy breeze penetrating his bones. Was she right?

Damn it, she'd only grown more beautiful, more appealing, more everything.

Now what was he going to do about it?

CHAPTER 6

"Hey Mom. Sure, I've got time. I'm just cooling down from my run." Cam unlocked his front door and stepped out of yet another downright freezing morning.

"Are you listening to me, Cameron Matthew?"

"Yes Mom, we can start up Sunday dinners again. I don't know if Campbell and Jack can drive up every week but at least once a month." Growing up and during college breaks, his mom always made Sunday dinner and the regularity and normalcy of it was something he'd missed during his decade abroad.

His parents had recently retired to nearby Pacific Grove and were eager to resume old family traditions. But he worried they had moved down from San Francisco because they assumed he needed help. Cam crossed to the chef's kitchen of his three-bedroom bungalow to brew coffee since he had tossed and turned all night.

"What else is new with me? Just busy at the hotel. Until launch day, that's where I'll be." No need to mention that his ex-girlfriend who his parents had adored was working for him.

His mom's voice lowered. "Cam, I want you to listen to what I'm going to say all the way through before you respond, okay?"

"Of course."

"Well, I was talking to an old friend who lives down in Laguna Beach and she works with the most incredible group called Pups-4-Vets. They save dogs from rescue groups and shelters and train them to be service animals."

"Mom, that's great but I don't need a service dog. I just ran five miles. I work long hours." He strode to the large bay window and glared at the lush green trees and the peek ocean view. Ignored the throbbing pain in his left thigh where it attached to his prosthetic.

His mom huffed a breath. "I asked you to let me finish."

"Sorry." He scrubbed a hand over his face. When would everyone stop trying to help him? Note to world, he was doing fine on his own.

"So, my friend knows about your injury and that you resigned your commission early and are running the hotel. She said she's got an incredible dog that's trained to work with someone just like you--"

His fingers clenched. "Just like me? What, disabled? Without a leg? I told you I'm rehabbed. I don't need a dog. Those dogs should go to someone who really needs them, someone in a wheelchair."

"Cameron Matthew Taylor, I asked you not to interrupt me and the dogs aren't just for people in wheelchairs. They are highly sensitive and are excellent companions for people dealing with posttraumatic stress, like nightmares and panic attacks. I know how independent you are. I know you are strong enough to handle everything on your own. But you don't have to."

A familiar hammering started in his forehead. "Mom, I--"

"Look sweetheart, just think about it. Everyone is happier with a pet. They reduce stress. They offer unconditional love. Don't you remember all the dogs we've had before? Your dog could run with you, go to the hotel with you, just be with you. I don't worry about your leg, Cam, I worry about your heart." Her voice softened.

Damn if that wasn't a direct hit. Especially adding in the complication of Lucy. He massaged his aching temples. His mom meant well. "I'm fine. I'm enjoying the challenge of the hotel and I'm lucky I get to work with my best friends, my life is full. I don't have time to look after a dog."

"Don't be silly. And there's something else--this dog isn't technically a service animal and needs a home pronto. He was kicked out the program halfway through because of some food issues."

"Issues with food?"

His mom chuckled. "Well, apparently, he did fine through most of training but then he had a few...ahem...incidents over Thanksgiving when a freshly cooked turkey was left up on a counter."

"So, you have a turkey thief who flunked out of training, and it sounds like you've already told your friend I'm taking the dog." Cam leaned against the wall, watching the clouds float across the stormy sky.

His mom had the grace to clear her throat. "Well, she's on her way up this morning and has Frank. And despite his penchant for poultry, he's a good boy. And like I said, they can't afford to keep him when they need to train new dogs."

"Frank? Seriously?" He snickered.

"It's a lovely name. Look, will you at least meet Frank? For me? See if you connect? And if you don't, there's no pressure to adopt him. I'm sure they'll find a lovely home for the poor boy." She was nothing if not persistent.

As if he could refuse her anything. "Well, it sounds like you have it all arranged anyway. I'll be at the hotel until noon but could meet up afterward."

"Mary and I will bring him out to the hotel. I'd love to see the progress. Say, 12:30?"

He winced. Lucy might be at the hotel and no way in hell was his mom going to see her. Not yet anyway. "No, it's chaotic out there with all the construction. It would be better to meet Frank here, where it's quiet."

"Okay, that's fine. And, by the way, the organization is a non-profit. Isn't that lovely?"

"Mom, I'm already meeting Frank. No need to keep selling him to me. But I'm not promising anything, okay? And let your friend know it is a very, very, very longshot."

"There's my favorite son. Of course, it's your call." Her tone held a hint of smugness.

He rolled his eyes. "I'm your only son, Mom."

"My favorite. See you later." She breezed off the call.

CAM PULLED into his driveway at 12:28 p.m. People used to give him crap that he was anal about punctuality, but the reality was his mom had drilled it into him. Despite her mild temperament, tardy people sparked her temper. He'd learned early on that nothing was worth being late in the Taylor household.

So, of course, his mom and her friend were already waiting inside the low white picket fence. He couldn't see the dog yet but braced himself for the full sales pitch. He hadn't heard a flurry of barking, so that was an instant plus.

And damn if he wasn't thinking like the dog was already his.

He squared his shoulders and opened the latched gate. "Hey Mom, Mary."

"Hi sweetie, you ready to meet the new love of your life?" His mom started to cross the verdant lawn toward him.

Lucy's face immediately popped into his brain, and he flinched. "You're awfully optimistic."

The tall brunette with his mom turned and whistled. "Frank."

A blur of tan and black fur flew around the side yard and skidded to a halt at Mary's feet.

Cam looked down at the medium sized shepherd mix and the dog stared up at him with enormous chocolate eyes, his black-nosed face tilted to the side.

The first thing he noticed was that Frank's ears stuck out perpendicular from his narrow face. Like, really perpendicular. Absurd, actually.

He couldn't help it, he burst out laughing. "What's with the rabbit ears?"

"He's had them since he was a pup. They make him look less intimidating. You know people can be scared by German Shepherds," Mary said.

Cam crossed to the dog and reached out a hand so Frank could sniff him. The dog smelled and then pushed his head up into Cam's hand, angling for a rubdown. Cam crouched next to the dog and scratched behind his ridiculous ears. Frank leaned his weight against him and his tail thumped wildly on the grass.

Cam glanced up at his mom's friend. "So, I hear he failed out of school for stealing Thanksgiving dinner?"

Mary's lips curved up. "It's not uncommon for even the best trained animals to have food issues. He's perfect in every other way but him lunging for a snack with a veteran who needs him for balance and support could be a real issue. We've got other dogs who would be wonderful service dogs but flunk out for other reasons, like early hip dysplasia or dog aggression. Frank is essentially the perfect dog, except for his relentless quest for treats."

"Look, I'm not sure what my Mom told you, but I really don't have time for a dog right now. I'm opening a new hotel and my schedule is hectic. I'm afraid you've wasted your time."

His Mom huffed out a breath. "Cameron, you haven't given Frank a chance. Why don't you take him for a spin around the block? We'll make some tea and wait for you on the back patio."

Frank popped up from his seated position, his feathery tail pumping in the air. So apparently he understood the term "walk."

From thirty-five years of experience, Cam knew not to argue with his mom. It would be easier to take the goofy dog on a walk and then let her down gently.

"Fine." He grabbed the leash and headed out of the yard. "We'll be back in ten minutes but I'm not going to change my mind." He latched the gate behind him. He had to get the last word in once in a while.

He turned down the sidewalk, Frank prancing along next to him, his tail wagging and his ears bouncing. "Okay, boy, you are one happy dog, I'll give you that."

Frank grinned up at him, then turned his attention to checking out the new and thrilling smells lurking in the grass and shrubs lining the sidewalk. The customary breeze held a hint of salt and not too much chill with the sun beaming down from the blue sky.

The dog marched at a perfect stride, like a well-trained soldier. Cam picked up the pace to a light jog and Frank happily matched him. When they turned the corner, another dog was approaching with one of Cam's neighbors. An older guy--Ben? Bob? Brian?

Frank's tail accelerated but he stayed in step.

"Hi there, Cameron. Name's Brian in case you forgot. About time you got a dog. Brutus here wants to say hi, is that okay?" The white-haired gentleman sporting a Member's Only jacket and faded jeans stopped and his little French bulldog vibrated with excitement when it spotted Frank.

Cam's lips twitched. A ten-pound dog named Brutus? "Well, this isn't my dog but Frank's well-trained, so sure, they can say hi."

The two dogs danced around each other, then moved on to the all-important butt sniff for approval. Tails wagged and they started to play.

"Oh, walking the dog for your girlfriend?" Brian winked.

Cam stiffened. "For my mom. She wants me to adopt him. But I'm too busy for a dog right now."

"You're never too busy for a dog. Young man like you? Take him to work with you. He and Brutus like each other, you could bring him over for play dates."

Play dates? He glanced down and the two dogs were basically rubbing cheeks. Okay, so Frank was charming and well-behaved. But Cam drew the line at play dates of any kind.

"Thanks. I better get back. You have a nice rest of your walk." He gave a half-wave and continued down the street.

"We'll be seeing you," The man called. "Bring Frank by any time."

He finished the quick stroll and returned to the house. Frank followed him inside and they reached the kitchen where his mom and Mary stood. His mom was arranging some crackers and cheese on a plate and had mugs of steaming tea ready. Frank's ears perked up and he raised his wet black nose and sniffed the air.

"No cheese for you, young man." Mary wagged a finger at him, but she was grinning.

"He likes cheese too?"

"It is a snack food, right? Don't worry, I brought some of his favorite dog biscuits. Let's go out back." His mom carried the tray and they all fell in line behind her.

Once they'd settled around the large outdoor table on his shaded back patio, Frank settled at his feet. Okay, the dog was pretty damn cute. And obedient.

"So how was your walk?" His mom raised her brows and popped a cube of cheese into her mouth.

"Fine."

She sighed. "Cameron. Was he a good boy? Did you enjoy his company? Can you see how having him around would make your house feel more like a home?"

"What's wrong with my house? Your daughter decorated it. Should I tell Campbell you don't approve of her interior design skills?" He liked his rental and when his sister had spent a few weeks with him last year, she'd transformed it from spartan man-cave to cozy Northern California beach chic. At least that's what she'd called it.

His mom grinned. "Don't you dare. Your place is great. It's just quiet. And you're quiet. I just think Frank would make life more fun for you."

Frank shifted his head so it was resting on Cam's foot and peered up at him, his silly ears defying gravity, his brown eyes hopeful. The animal knew they were discussing him.

Before he could answer, Mary leaned her elbows on the table. "I have a proposition for you. Will you foster Frank for two weeks? It would really help the rescue out. They're over-whelmed right now with all the dogs they're training and that way we won't have to put him in a kennel until another foster home opens up."

He sucked in a breath. "Foster?" He gazed down into

Frank's soulful eyes. This dog didn't belong in a cage. Well, no dog did. Something tugged in his chest.

"It would really help us out. And that way you could see if Frank fits into your life. If at the end of the two weeks, it just doesn't work, you'll have made a huge difference for Pups-4-Vets."

He glanced up at his mom and she nodded, her gaze hopeful. "Your father and I can help out if you really need it."

"Why don't you guys take Frank? You've got your new house, you're retired, you've got all the time in the world. Doesn't that make more sense?" Probably because they thought he needed the companionship. And maybe they were right.

She shook her head. "We'll do that at some point but we're in the midst of this big transition, so the timing isn't right. But we could walk Frank or take him for a day if you really needed it."

He reached down and rubbed Frank's soft fur and the dog turned and kissed his hand and batted his eyelashes. Damn it.

"Two weeks. And I'll have your word that if it doesn't work out for any reason at all, you will take Frank back." He looked between the two women.

Mary reached a hand across the table and gave his a firm shake. "Deal. Now I've got his bed, food, and some toys in the car." She rose from the table and headed back through the house.

He narrowed his eyes at his mom. "Huh."

"Being prepared is important, right?" She flashed a grin, her blue eyes twinkling.

"Why do I feel like I got played?"

Her smile disappeared. "Cam, we didn't play you. And Frank doesn't feel like a service dog, right? He just feels like a pet. Mary did need a foster for him, and she will take him if you don't want to keep him, okay?"

He squeezed his eyes shut for a minute. When had he gotten so damn defensive? His mom loved him and had always looked out for him and his sisters. And yeah, it was an adjustment to live alone after all the years in the Army. Frank bumped against him, and he reached down to scratch the dog's head. Just having the furry guy leaning into him lowered his blood pressure. "Yeah. He's pretty cute. And you're right, it is quiet here."

His phone vibrated. "Well, except the work calls never end." He fished the phone out of his jacket pocket and immediately recognized the number––Lucy. He hadn't programmed her in his phone yet.

"Do you need to take that?"

He shook his head. "It's just a text from the new wedding planner."

"Wedding planner?" His mom cocked her head.

He nodded while reading Lucy's text alerting him the Harringtons had already reviewed the proposal, thought it looked good, and would give them their decision by the end of the week.

"Yeah, we're marketing Cypress Coast Ranch as the new wedding venue on the Monterey Peninsula. There's stiff competition and I've got to make sure my hotel can be as profitable as the rest of our properties. Ryan and Charlie hired someone to handle the weddings and events full-time." He swallowed the guilt at not telling his mom *who* the new hire was. He wasn't ready for that discussion.

"I'd imagine you've got a lot of competition with the Pebble Beach Golf Course and that fancy Portola Hotel."

His eyes widened. "You've only been down here a month, and you already know about wedding venues?" His mom wanted her three children married sooner than later. Luckily, Campbell had recently gotten engaged to his best friend and honorary brother, Jack. That should keep his mom off his case for a while.

She shrugged. "Well, Campbell's not sure where she wants to get married, and I know Charlie and Ryan are tying the knot at your hotel. I don't want Camille to marry that guy she's still seeing. And all the wedding talk with Campbell got me thinking about something…" Her lips curved up.

"Do I want to know?" Had his mom always been such a strategic planner? She played a hell of a game of chess but now that she'd retired from teaching, who knew what she'd plot with all the additional time.

She pressed one hand to her heart. "Your father and I want to renew our vows. You know we eloped, and we thought it would be lovely to have a real wedding."

His heart warmed. His parents had been happy together for as long as he could remember. They were true partners and although they had arguments and different views on things, they were devoted to each other. More importantly, they had fun together and made the Taylor house warm, welcoming, and supportive. Was that what Lucy had wanted for them?

"Cam, are you listening to me?" His mom's voice rose.

He rubbed his jaw. "Sorry, what?"

"Can you give me the wedding planner's number? That way I won't have to bug you asking questions about having our renewal ceremony there."

"Are you sure? We're booked for most of the year." Cam's breath caught in his throat. It was a miracle his sister hadn't already told their mom about it but maybe Campbell hadn't wanted to interfere.

Her brow furrowed. "Why are you being weird? I'm exploring all the options. And I thought you'd be thrilled not to have to talk about weddings with me."

He ran his tongue around his teeth. "Well, there's something you should know. I don't want to have a big discussion around it, okay?"

"Okay?"

"The original wedding planner quit at the last minute and recommended a replacement. It's Lucy." The words tumbled out in a rush.

"Lucy?" She tilted her head.

"Lucy. Lucy Goodwin. Lucy, my ex." He rubbed the tight cords on the back of his neck.

Her lips parted and her eyes rounded. "Lucy Goodwin? She's a wedding planner? Here in Monterey? Working with you? How in the world?"

He threw up his hands. "That's what I said. What are the odds, right?"

His mom paused, leaned back in her chair, and sipped her tea. "Is she good?"

"Good?" Good-looking? Good person? Good kisser? Yes, yes, yes.

"Is she good at her job? She had the sunniest disposition and every person who met her adored her, like we did. But wedding planning is a very stressful career."

He sighed. "We had a meeting a few days ago with some family that is supposed to be the wedding of the century or something. A big influencer. And Mom, Lucy was incredible. So prepared and engaged. These people are a pain in the butt from what I saw, and she just handled them. Ryan and Charlie were there too, and they were blown away. I guess this wedding could give our hotel a major advantage and put us on the map."

His mom clasped her hands together. "That's wonderful. And how is she? How did she look? How's her health?"

Cam's chest tightened. "She seems great." *She looked drop dead gorgeous and tasted delicious.*

"Is she married? Kids?"

"No." He gritted his teeth.

"Hmm…she's single. You're single. You're both in Monterey. You're both working together." She smiled slyly and ticked the points off with her fingers.

He frowned. "Mom."

She waved a hand. "I mean, look at your two best friends. Ryan and Jack both worked with Charlie and Campbell…"

He shook his head. "Don't get any ideas, okay?"

"I just think it seems like fate's stepping in and giving you a second chance to get it right, that's all." She raised her eyebrows.

He opened his mouth to disagree. To vehemently disagree but Mary returned through the patio's sliding glass doors. Thank god.

"Okay, I put the bed next to the couch and all Frank's food and things are in the box on the kitchen island. I can't thank you enough." Mary smiled and glanced down at where the dog snoozed at his feet.

Cam rose and Frank scrambled up to sit next to him. "We'll see how it goes. I've got to get back to the hotel and I guess he's coming with me."

Who was he kidding? Frank was going to be his dog. He just wouldn't admit he'd capitulated so fast. Not yet.

His mom stood and gave him a one-armed hug. "It'll be great, you'll see. Now please give me Lucy's number and we'll get out of your hair."

He sighed. "Fine. But you keep the discussion to your and dad's ceremony, okay? Please?"

"So, I'd like to invite her to the next Sunday dinner for old time's sake." She squeezed his shoulder.

He jolted. "No." If he hadn't been able to resist kissing her, he certainly wasn't ready to see her with his family again.

"Really? Don't you think it's a good idea since you'll be

working together? She was like a daughter to me. And to your dad too."

He grimaced––his mom knew how to layer on the guilt. "Fine."

She scurried past him and preceded him into the house. "See you two later. Have fun with Frank."

Cam followed them out to the front yard and waved goodbye. His stomach was in knots—he knew his mom meant well but her calling Lucy was going to create trouble. Like he needed more complications.

CHAPTER 7

"Mrs. Taylor? Oh, my goodness, I can't believe it's you." Lucy adjusted her ear buds and pressed one hand to her heart. She'd adored Cam's parents and losing them after the break-up had only magnified her pain.

"Oh Lucy, when Cameron told me you just started as the new wedding planner at his hotel? I couldn't wait to call you. Even if Clyde and I weren't looking to renew our vows, I'd have called. How are you?" Christine Taylor's voice burst with genuine emotion.

Lucy rose from her ergonomically correct desk chair and tossed herself onto her marshmallow soft couch. She'd spent the morning with her nose buried in spreadsheets for what felt like countless upcoming events. Somehow it was already 4:15. Sue was coming over at 5 with take-out and a bottle of wine.

"I'm great. Playing catch up with everything booked prior to my coming on board." Although her brain was over-flowing with data on ruby vs. garnet, classic vs. farmhouse, and all the choices and themes.

"Is now a bad time? Shall I call you back later?"

"No, your timing is perfect. I need a break. So, you're looking to renew your vows at Cypress Coast Ranch? I think that's lovely. Did you have a time in mind?" Lucy reclined into the fluffy cushions and propped her feet up.

"We're flexible. We're just settling in to Pacific Grove because we decided to retire early and enjoy life living closer to Cameron and Campbell."

Lucy tucked a strand of hair behind her ear. "Oh wow, that's lovely. Campbell's in Paso Robles with Jack, right? Where is Camille these days? Did she relocate to Central California too?"

"Camille is still up in San Francisco, but she travels a great deal for work. And I'm thrilled that Campbell and Jack are engaged and based a few hours south. But tell me how you ended up on the Central Coast and working with Cameron?" Mrs. T's voice was warm.

"Well, I started doing weddings straight out of college. About six years ago I spent a year in Kauai working at a wedding destination hotel, which I loved. I really wanted to find the best of both worlds––so I returned to California and am thrilled to have found a role as resident wedding planner." One part purpose and one part destiny?

"That's wonderful. Your parents must be so proud. Are they still in the Bay Area?"

Lucy ran her tongue around her teeth. "They are, but of course my dad wishes I still lived with them. You remember how over-protective he can be." If the man could wrap her in cotton wool and keep her on a shelf like a doll, he'd try.

"Well, that's understandable on his part after everything you went through. Cameron accused us of the same thing when we moved down here. But like you, he's used to taking care of himself."

"That's the truth." Himself and only himself.

"Well, it sounds like it was meant to be. I'm thrilled, and I can't wait to see you again, Lucy. And I'm so happy you're healthy."

Lucy nibbled on her lower lip. Meant to be--more like meant to disrupt her life. "Thanks. And I'm looking forward to seeing you too. It really is all a coincidence, and the job is an opportunity of a lifetime." What she'd worked for and dreamt of for years.

"Well, I'm not going to ask how it's going with my son. At least right now. But I'd love it if we could set up a meeting to talk about squeezing us in to the schedule for a renewal celebration. I know you're probably incredibly busy but maybe we could have coffee or lunch?" Mrs. T's voice was hopeful.

"I'd love to. My schedule this week is completely full, but I could do next Tuesday for coffee or Wednesday for lunch?" Maybe she'd have built up more of a protective shell where Cam was concerned by then. *Ha.*

"Let's meet over at Plumes for coffee and breakfast Tuesday. Does 8 o'clock work?"

The charming coffeehouse was a popular spot in Monterey. "Absolutely. I love their breakfast sandwiches. I'm looking forward to it."

"Me too, sweetie. Oh, Clyde's going to be thrilled when I tell him we're getting together."

They rang off. Lucy dropped the phone on the sofa and leaned her head back into the comfy upholstery. Her eyelids drifted shut and she massaged her temples. If anyone had told her she'd be coming full circle seeing the Taylors again and spending her days with Cam, she wouldn't have believed it.

Vivid memories flooded through her, clear, like they'd happened yesterday and not more than a decade ago. She and Cam going for long runs, followed by cozy evenings listening to classic rock and roll, and talking for hours late into the night. Although Cam wasn't the most social guy, with her, he'd felt comfortable and they'd discuss everything from their favorite historical fiction to global politics, to dreams of the future. A future she'd believed they'd share.

He'd been her first love and she'd believed he'd be her one and only.

And then she'd spent years trying to find someone who wanted the full deal--marriage, family, all of it. Tried to replace Cameron. Apparently, she had a thing for handsome blond men with raspy voices. She'd cared deeply about the three other men who came into her life but none of them were Cam. Hence, her dismal record of returning diamond rings.

Engagement Number 1 was to another aloof yet charismatic man or Cam 2.0.

Engagement Number 2 was to Thomas who devolved into a controlling jerk.

Engagement Number 3 was to Greg, who was the nicest person she'd ever met but just hadn't been right for her. After breaking up with him a few years back, she'd broken her unhealthy pattern and focused solely on her career.

But Cam's confession he'd spoken with her dad had blindsided her. Maybe if he hadn't encouraged Cam to break up with her, she could have had it all. Who said having true love and her dream career had to be mutually exclusive?

She'd managed to restrain herself from calling her dad and letting him have it. Although she loved her parents, her dad's inability to believe she could stand on her own two feet stung. But she knew she had a quick fuse and any time she reacted from anger or pain, she usually regretted it. She'd learned to give herself a few days to cool down before responding.

And this ability had probably saved her every single wedding client from the beginning of her career. Brides tended to call twenty-four/seven, operating in panic mode for most of their wedding planning. Any potential snag was seen as epic and blown out of proportion. No need to act like a bridezilla in her own life. Especially since she'd never personally made it to the altar.

All the while, she excelled at helping other people create their perfect weddings. Ironic. And here she was in a new role as the resident wedding planner working for the man who started it all. She blew out a breath. No time to wallow in it right now. She refused to be a wallower.

Lucy glanced at her watch and popped off the couch. Time to change into her favorite ratty burgundy sweats, light some candles, set up the streaming café lounge music and make sure the cottage was welcoming. Tonight, she'd share everything with Sue and get her best friend's stellar advice.

Sue burst through the front door, in all her 6 feet of sarcastic fiery glory, her arms full of delicious smelling bags. "I battled gale force winds and just missed tonight's storm, but I've come with all your favorite treats, sourced from not one, not two, but three of our favorite restaurants, including El Cantaro."

"You're the best. I don't care what anyone says." Lucy grinned and crossed to help her friend carry in the loot.

Sue placed the bags on the small butcher block kitchen island and pulled Lucy in for a tight hug. "Ha-ha. Very funny. Tonight, we will feast on all your favorite comfort foods, washed down with a delicious Washington Cabernet I've been saving. And you will give me all the details about working with your ex."

Lucy's shoulders relaxed. "Sounds like a plan. And his mom called me today and we're having coffee next week so I can help her plan a renewal of vows with Cam's dad. It's all feeling surreal."

"Surreal is right. I want to hear all about your walk and

talk." Sue slid the wine opener out of the drawer and removed the cork with a flourish.

Lucy grabbed a wineglass, poured, and downed a healthy gulp.

"Hey, that needs to breathe for a while, you heathen." Sue wagged a finger.

"Sorry, but I needed it. Don't tell the wine police. Or Cam's sister Campbell, who is studying to be a Master Sommelier. Everything's moving so fast." Liquid courage and all that.

Sue's dark brows knit together over her adorable ski-jump nose. "Never fear, that's why I'm here. We'll strategize over chips and guac. By the time we polish off the cannoli and this excellent bottle of wine, you'll have a plan."

Lucy's stomach did a little flip. "Okay."

Her mouth watered as she pulled the tray of fragrant lasagna out and placed the foil-wrapped dish in the oven to stay warm, then stowed the cannoli in the refrigerator. "Thank you for getting the giant serving of chips and guacamole. I'll need these." Mexican and Italian were her favorite and tonight she'd definitely be eating her feelings.

"We also won't be telling your sommelier friend about the Cabernet and chip combination. Pretty sure that won't be on the food pairings at any of the fancy hotel restaurants." Sue carried over the ginormous platter to the coffee table and sank onto the L-shaped camel-colored couch.

Lucy dipped a still-warm tortilla chip into the chunky guacamole that El Cantaro was famous for. She moaned when she bit into it, the contrast of crunch and creaminess the perfect combination.

"It will be our secret. And if we could only discover their secret guac recipe, we could make it at home and never leave the house." She joined her friend on the couch.

Sue chuckled. "You'd go bananas in a few days without social time. But I hear you."

They nibbled for a few minutes, allowing the deep ruby wine time to breathe and open up. It would be perfect when they moved to the pasta portion of their evening.

Lucy tucked her legs beneath her and angled to face her best friend. "Thanks for picking up dinner. How's everything going with the renovation?"

"I'm not sure why I thought it would be such a good idea to get into flipping houses. Because my first one is going to be a flip-fail." Sue glared at the dish of chips.

"You got into it because you're a kick-ass realtor and you also happen to have an incredible eye for design. Not to mention you are talented at bossing around crews of people. So why is it a fail?"

Sue pursed her lips and blew out a breath. "Because I'm in love with the house and I don't want to sell it. I want to keep it for myself. So, I'm a failure. You know, like when people foster animals and end up adopting them because they grow too attached?"

Lucy threw back her head and laughed. "You are not a failure. If you love the house, keep it. You can use it as an example of your talents and just flip the next one. Besides the convenience of you being a few blocks away makes me happy."

"Huh." Sue shook her head, her springy chestnut curls bouncing. "You always see the silver lining. I don't know how you do it."

Lucy shrugged. "Not always. But with you it's easy to see."

Sue waved one hand. "Okay, enough about me and my many weaknesses. Let's discuss Cameron Taylor. The man, the myth, the legend. I cannot wait to meet him again to see if he lives up to all the stories you told me. But first tell me you're okay?"

Lucy bit her lip. "I am okay, but I still can't actually believe it. Everything happened so fast when Joy asked me to interview."

"And you really had no idea Cam was in Monterey?"

She shook her head. "Why would I? Much less out of the Army and running a hotel. Then when I found out, I figured I could handle it. I mean, it's my dream job, it fell into my lap, and it's been more than a decade. A lot has happened since then."

Sue raised her eyebrows. "Okay, that's the logical brain talking, what about your heart? How did you feel when you saw Cameron for the first time?"

Lucy's eyes closed and she rubbed her heart. "Like I was going to throw up the tuna sandwich I'd just had for lunch. Then it felt like the first time I saw him when I was fourteen years old. Like a lightning strike through my heart. And then it was strange because in one way it felt like it was only yesterday since I saw him last but then it was different. *He* was different."

Sue reached over and rubbed her shoulder. "Oh girl, I bet. You've both navigated your twenties and he lived through war. You know I don't believe in all that woo-woo nonsense about soul mates and fate but even this great skeptic finds your situation to be curious."

"Curious is a good word for it. I mean, he was supposed to stay in the military forever––he chose it over me. Basically said it wouldn't be fair to me because he couldn't do both. So, the odds of him running a luxury hotel and me working for him, in a town neither of us had a connection with before now..." A shiver sparked down her spine.

Sue's brows drew together. "Are you still attracted to him?"

"Yeah. If anything, he's more attractive now," Lucy sighed. "But he's more closed off. He lost his lower leg, and he chose to resign his commission. War changes a person. But at his core, I'm sure he is the same Cameron, just like I'm the same person, just without the rose-colored spectacles."

"Wow, that's tough for him. Who knows what hell he experienced over there? Both of you have been through a lot. Do you think you could ever trust him again?"

"Trust? You mean not to break my heart if we tried again?" Lucy's heartrate kicked up.

Sue nodded. "You've thought about it, haven't you? I know he was everything to you and none of your other relationships could compare."

"If only I hadn't gone so far as to get engaged three times––not sure what I was thinking." Lucy picked up her wine and took a long sip. "We met for a walk and hashed through the past. He pointed something out I hadn't considered. He said he thought I had our future mapped out and he needed to discover the world on his own first. So maybe he wasn't the only one at fault..." And didn't that change her narrative?

Sue's eyes narrowed. "We agreed you'd stop beating yourself up for those break-ups. You wanted to love all three of them more than you did. It's not like you jilted them at the altar or divorced them after three months or something. Anyway, like Cam blamed you?"

"No, he didn't blame me. But I did see our future so clearly and had assumed he did too. I knew he was my forever person." She'd buried that conviction deep inside the locked chamber in her heart.

Sue's brow furrowed. "Huh. Well, if he'd discussed it instead of just dumping you flat, maybe you guys could have worked it out. Did you two set some ground rules on your walk?"

"Ground rules?"

Sue waved a chip. "Well yeah. Like, you agree to be civil

co-workers. Or friends. Or friends with benefits. Or go for a second chance. You should kiss him and see what happens."

Heat flooded Lucy's cheeks. "Kiss him?"

"Yes, Ms. Parrot. It would be one way to see where you both stand, right?"

Lucy blew out a shaky breath and rose from the couch. "I did kiss him. And the chemistry is still there."

"Oh, when were you going to tell me that? Talk about burying the lede." Sue's eyes widened.

"I'm still processing it. I'm going to get the lasagna." Lucy stalked to the kitchen island and worked to regulate her breath. She wasn't ready to share the details of their first kiss in thirteen years. Because remembering the feel of his beautiful mouth on hers sent the blood coursing through her veins and hope fluttering in her belly.

It couldn't simply be coincidence that they'd been reunited at Cypress Coast Ranch, could it?

CHAPTER 8

Cam surveyed the newly renovated solo loft and nodded in satisfaction. Of Cypress Coast Ranch's ten converted farm buildings, the small room with the wood-burning fireplace and private patio was his favorite. Tranquil, quiet, and created with the single traveler in mind, it was perfect. Or at least he'd thought so until that kiss with Lucy. Why did the romantic honeymoon suite appeal to him now?

The eight-bedroom bunkhouse and the handful of one-to-three-bedroom structures allowed guests to reserve an intimate retreat or book a space for family and friends. The set-up was one of the unique features that distinguished his hotel from other Monterey Peninsula luxury resorts. It was also ideal for wedding parties and guests or so everyone told him.

Last Fall when Pacific Jewel Inn opened, the team started the "spend the night" tradition. The inaugural night in La Jolla was great but the first night at Maison du Soleil in Paso Robles had been one of his toughest days since he landed stateside.

He'd been toasting the success of their two new properties with the team when Charlie broke the news she was interviewing Lucy. The shock at hearing his ex's name and learning she lived in Monterey had thrust him into a spiral. He'd fled to his fancy room and drowned his mood in a bottle of Jameson. All that idiotic move had accomplished was triggering flashback-filled nightmares of Afghanistan. Not exactly helpful for his recovery.

He gritted his teeth and squeezed his eyes closed. No dwelling on the past. No resurrecting feelings that he'd buried years ago. Despite their talk at the beach and the kiss that reminded him no woman could hold a candle to Lucy, he needed to uphold his boundaries around her. Cypress Coast Ranch was the priority and he'd make Lucy feel safe and comfortable working for him if it killed him.

No more reminiscing about the past.

No more getting together outside of work.

Well, unless she accepted his mom's invitation to next Sunday's dinner. At least he'd have the buffer of Jack and Campbell and could avoid being alone with Lucy.

Lucy deserved a great guy who could give her everything she deserved, and that guy wasn't a scarred veteran with PTSD. He needed to accept he couldn't be anything but her boss.

His phone dinged and he grimaced at the screen. The Harringtons. Again. Those damn women were relentless. In addition to calling Lucy several times a day, they'd started pestering him too. Like he had any clue about flowers and color schemes.

Until he spoke with them, they'd continue hammering away. May as well get it over with. "Cameron Taylor."

"Hello Cameron, it's Pamela Harrington. You're not an easy man to get a hold of." Her nasally voice held a hint of reproach.

He cleared his throat. "What can I do for you?" *How can I stop you from ever calling me again?*

"I just got off the phone with Lucy. She's just a joy to work with." She paused long enough to convey that he was not. "We are very close to making a decision and Victoria and I want to come out one more time and walk through. We'll need both of you to be there."

Cam gritted his teeth. "Lucy is excellent at her job and is authorized to handle all contract negotiations." He'd rather work with his partner Lucas on spreadsheets and financials––anything would be better than another meeting with who Lucy called "bridezilla."

"Of course she is. But we want both of you. After all, you are the face of Cypress Coast Ranch, aren't you? We just need to be 1,000 percent sure we're making the right decision and we just couldn't possibly commit to it without you. You understand, don't you?"

In other words, we've got you by the short hairs and you will do as I say. This woman could have excelled in the military. She'd accept no opposition. If the family was as influential as Lucy, Ryan, and Charlie claimed, he needed to suck it up. He bit the inside of his cheek to stem a groan. How had he gone from being a respected commanding officer in the Army to a lowly plebe jumping through hoops?

"Absolutely. Did you want to set something up for next week?" It was Friday at 4 p.m. and visions of settling on the couch with Frank, zoning out to ESPN and a pizza with all the toppings had gotten him through the day. He needed the break because this weekend was work, work, and more work.

"Oh no. Victoria can't wait. We're here in town and our driver is picking us up now. We can be there in twenty minutes." The woman had the nerve to chuckle.

Not a question. Not a request. A damn ambush. If this

was how the hospitality business worked, maybe he'd miscalculated because this was bullshit.

"Great. I'll meet you in the ballroom." He looked down at his faded jeans and old San Francisco Giants t-shirt. The Harringtons would just have to deal with his "image."

"Excellent. We're picking up Lucy, so we'll see you in a few minutes." The woman hung up.

Picking up Lucy? What the hell? They'd steamrolled her too. If this woman did not sign a contract today and have her wedding here and get them a shit ton of business, he'd be pissed.

Frank rubbed against his legs, reminding him the bride-to-be probably wouldn't welcome a big hairy beast along for the tour. The dog already had him wrapped around his paw. Frank was the perfect companion––he loved long walks, snuggling on the couch, and not talking. Or barking. But now he needed to move Frank from his office to the back of his Jeep, even though the picture of Frank galloping up to the Harringtons, had him smirking.

His smile faded. He hadn't planned on seeing Lucy for a few days. Time to rebuild his defenses that had crumbled with one kiss. Each time he saw Lucy, another long-buried image would pop up in his mind––anything from the way she tilted her head or narrowed her sparkling dark eyes when she was listening to you. Lucy had a way of making you feel like you were the only person in the world. Her ability to intensely concentrate on whoever she was engaged with was part of what made her so special.

And having to see her again now was a visceral reminder that their long-ago chemistry was no fluke. The curve of her waist, the fullness of her lower lip, the lemony scent that was a part of her and brought him back to the days when she was his.

A sharp jolt lanced through him. He shoved his memories

back into the vault and slammed the locks home. Thank god he had years of practice of looking non-reactive. He'd need it.

~

"OF COURSE, Cameron views you both as important potential clients." Lucy laid a palm on Victoria's slender forearm. "But between you and me, running a business, being an exemplary leader, and managing the renovation are more in his comfort zone than weddings." And oh, she could bet he was beyond annoyed to be railroaded into this meeting today.

The bride-to-be sniffed. "I certainly hope so. I hope he realizes how much my position can influence business at your hotel. But I see your point––my fiancé wants nothing to do with the wedding planning. He just wants to show up."

Pamela brandished her champagne flute. "Men. But Cameron can certainly take the time for Victoria's wedding if he really cares about the success of the resort."

Lucy looked down and rifled through her satchel because she wasn't sure she could maintain a smile. The egos on these women were over-the-top. They'd leased a stretch limousine to whisk them from the airport where they'd flown in on a private jet. They'd decided to fly down to see the hotel again and only notified Lucy when they were in the air. On a forty-five-minute flight. Because of course nobody had any priorities over them. It was the clients like this that sometimes caused her to question her career choice.

But usually, once the big day came around, all the stress and theatrics that came before ended up being worth it. Seeing the joy on the bride and groom's faces and knowing she'd had a part in making their special day the best it could be was incredibly rewarding. Fingers crossed the Harrington wedding be worth all the drama.

The limo purred to a halt in front of the main building, which housed the ballroom and where Cam would be awaiting their arrival. *This should be interesting.* The chauffer opened the door and Lucy waved Victoria and Pamela out first. She gathered her composure and silently repeated *wedding of the decade, wedding of the decade* like some wedding planner training school mantra. She knew she'd be able to smile through the meeting, but she wasn't as confident about Cam maintaining his poker face.

Hopefully, he'd allow her to lead and just look handsome and act like the Harringtons were Very Important People, emphasis on Very. He'd been born to boss people around with minimal words and glacial looks, but his military career was over and now he had to learn to step back and be second in command once in a while.

She smothered a giggle. Maybe this afternoon would be more fun than she anticipated.

She joined the Harringtons and they crossed to the enormous glass entrance doors. Cam pulled them open, gesturing for them to enter the welcoming reception area. High ceilings with mahogany-wood-beams and expansive bay windows gave the rustic building an open yet warm atmosphere. Black and white framed photographs of the original farm and grounds adorned the pale cream walls. Unlike many of the other structures that had to be gutted and completely renovated, the main lodge had only needed a facelift.

"Welcome back to Cypress Coast Ranch Pamela, Victoria. I thought we'd start out at the beach first since the sun will be setting soon. Does that work for you?" Cameron nodded to each woman. Although he didn't remotely come close to effusiveness, he managed to come across as professional and a hint warmer than polite.

Lucy met his arctic blue eyes and gave a tiny nod. She'd

caught his glance at the four-inch patent-leather stiletto boots Victoria was sporting. Yeah, he still rocked his poker face.

Victoria nodded. "That's perfect. You know my preference is to be as close to the water as possible."

Her mother disagreed. "Your heels are going to trip you in the sand. I told you to wear flats."

"As if." Victoria rolled her eyes, turned to Lucy, and pointed at her feet. "Lucy, what size shoe do you wear?"

Lucy's eyes widened. "Um, I wear a 7." *Seriously?*

"Close enough. Thanks so much." Victoria strode to the bench against the far wall, sat, and stripped off her thigh-high boots.

"How is she going to accompany us to the beach and answer our questions without shoes?" Pamela pursed her lips.

"Well, we've got Cameron and video chat, of course. We'll come back here before we go into the gardens––those have pavers––and she can join us there." Victoria had it all figured out.

Resigned to her fate, Lucy crossed the lobby and handed over her sensible, low-heeled boots to Victoria. The kind most people wear in January when it's cold and blustery outside. At least her socks were a festive daisy pattern and didn't sport a single hole.

In the more than ten years she'd been a wedding planner, she'd escorted intoxicated guests out of receptions, cut one bride's bangs ten minutes before the woman walked down the aisle, and even donned a chartreuse taffeta dress to stand in for a hungover bridesmaid. Giving up her shoes was a first.

Lucy met Cam's eyes met again, and when his lips twitched, she managed not to burst out laughing. Between

Victoria commandeering her shoes like *that* was normal behavior, to admitting that Lucy didn't actually have to physically be at the property for this impromptu meeting, the afternoon was bordering on the absurd.

She and Cam had always been able to communicate without speaking a word. That connection remained intact despite the last several years. His displeasure at having to handle the Harringtons on his own was clear to her, but the two potential clients were oblivious.

Wedding of the decade. Wedding of the decade. It had to be worth it.

Victoria stood and wrinkled her patrician nose down at her borrowed boots. "They're a little snug but let's get this over with. I'll buzz you as soon as we're on the sand, Lucy."

Lucy flashed a bright smile. "I'll be ready." Victoria better not stretch out her Italian leather boots. They might not be Louboutins but she'd purchased them on a trip to Florence and they were one of her favorite pairs.

Cam glanced back over his broad shoulder, his eyes narrowed, his nostrils flared, like an angry bull. Lucy stifled another giggle. His expression reminded her of the time in high school when he'd had to accompany her to her cousin's baby shower.

After three excruciating hours of baby games, oohing and aahing over every gift, spanning from bibs to rattles to pink ruffled skirts, he'd lost his composure and stormed out of the house. Even in high school he'd been reserved but that day, he'd snapped.

And they'd only begun the afternoon tour. Hopefully today wouldn't last three hours. She couldn't afford for Cam to turn on his heel and jeopardize this deal.

At least Victoria hadn't asked to wear his boots. She swallowed a snort.

Her phone buzzed and she answered with a smile. "How is it out there?"

"It's freezing. This wind is biting through my shearling coat and even with these boots, I'm slipping and sliding in the sand. As I would never wear flats on my wedding day, I don't see how this could possibly work unless you put out flooring or something." Victoria grimaced.

Flooring? On the beach? Was she kidding with this? "Well, what works well is a walkway that leads to the pergola or archway, with the chairs framing either side. So guests will end up with their feet in the sand, but you could have that support beneath you the entire way if you prefer."

Pamela's head appeared next to her daughter's. "Well, I don't want to have my heel stuck in the sand. Cameron suggested going barefoot, could you imagine?"

Lucy bit her lip. Of course he had. Because most people did end up barefoot on the beach. It was quite a thing. But obviously not Victoria Harrington's thing. Time to get the afternoon back on track.

"The aisle could be expanded to include the archway and all that area with a level base, including the front row where the family would sit. But again, the beach is only one option. There's enough room for your guests and you'll be getting married in the summer so it shouldn't be chilly--it's a personal preference," Lucy replied.

"Well, what do you suggest?" Victoria arched a ruthlessly groomed eyebrow.

Lucy smiled into the screen. "Cameron has an excellent point that many people like to get married with their toes in the sand. If that's not your inclination and you still prefer to be outdoors, the water views, and a hint of the sea breeze, I think the gardens might be a better fit. If you'll come back inside and get your shoes, we can go out there together."

"Well, I am not going barefoot while wearing haute

couture so that rules out one of three." Victoria powered off the phone.

Had the woman not pondered this before? Why would she consider a beach wedding if she didn't want to actually be in the sand? Lucy blew out a breath, stood and smoothed down her cashmere sweater set and wool slacks, ready to recoup her boots and get on with the wedding tour, take two.

The Harringtons and Cam swept into the lobby and Victoria strode over to the bench. "Thanks for lending me your shoes, they are actually kind of cute."

"Of course. Let's head back outside. I have a great feeling about the gardens for you." She crossed her fingers and zipped up her boots.

Victoria looped her arm through Lucy's. "I do too."

They sailed out the front door, leaving a granite-faced Cameron to escort Pamela.

Fortunately, the gardens had stone walkways so the clicking of Victoria's heels emphasized that she could, indeed, wear bridal stilts if she chose.

"So, we've got all these trees and flowering shrubs which will be in full bloom in June, but the florist can work miracles by bringing in whatever flowers you'd like. We can also have fairy lights strung through all the greenery to give you the princess-y vibe you wanted."

Victoria spun around and clasped her mother's arm. "This is it. I want to have the ceremony here in these gardens. Then have tables set up out here for dinner and dancing in the ballroom."

Cam's gaze met hers in the deepening twilight. She returned his look with a silent prayer that this was it.

Pamela nodded and they turned to Lucy. "Yes, this will be perfect. We'll need a detailed contract."

"Of course. I can put that together for you, and handle the

deposit once we confirm the menu, décor, music, and such. When would work best for you ladies?"

"Well, we've got dinner reservations tonight with some friends in Carmel and we're simply booked for the next several days. How about Wednesday afternoon?" Victoria was already scrolling through her phone.

Lucy was scheduled from 7 a.m. to 8 p.m. on Wednesday but she'd make room for this important meeting. "Absolutely. Let's do 1 p.m."

Cam finally spoke. "On behalf of Cypress Coast Ranch, I'd like to say thank you and we're thrilled to have you hold your wedding here. I've got a few out-of-town meetings, but I trust Lucy can handle everything here."

Did he now? She couldn't blame him for scheduling them now just to avoid the women.

"1 p.m. is fine. I'll bring my checkbook. And Lucy, can you find your way home? We've got to hurry to meet our friends. Can't be late for dinner." Pamela flashed a smile, already starting to walk out the door.

Force her to ride in the limo, take her boots, and then dump her? *No words.* "Oh, no problem. Have a lovely evening."

Once the front door closed behind them, she and Cam turned to look at each other and burst into laughter simultaneously.

"I'm happy to give you a ride home and buy you a pizza. As long as I don't have to ever see those women again. Promise me." Cam shuddered.

Lucy doubled over. "Wedding of the decade. Think of all the business. Think how envious all the other local wedding venues will be when they learn we're hosting the wedding of the decade. But I'll do my best."

"Then let's get out of here. I've got the dog in my Jeep and he may have already started eating the seatbelts or some-thing." Cam grinned, his expression soft, his eyes twinkling.

Cam was always handsome, but when he smiled and appeared happy? He was devastating. Heat pooled in her belly--her attraction to Cam hadn't diminished one bit but she could handle a ride home and a casual meal with him without her heart becoming involved.

Of course she could.

CHAPTER 9

"Oh my goodness, Frank is the sweetest dog I've ever met." Lucy buried her face in the animal's tan and black fur. The dog's tail thumped happily on the hardwood floor.

"Yeah, he's a happy boy," Cam said, something tightening in his chest at the picture Lucy and Frank made.

"I've wanted to get a pet forever but haven't because of my hours. I didn't think it would be fair. You'll bring him to work most days, right?"

He nodded. "Looks that way. I'll just have to keep him away from the restaurant. And speaking of food, I'm starving. Do you still like your pizza with pepperoni, or have you branched out?"

She wrinkled her nose at him. "Are you judging me? Pepperoni pizza is delicious. Why would I want to smother my beautiful cheese and sauce and crust with all kinds of things that don't belong there. Please tell me you don't still order pineapple on yours."

"Pineapple is high in antioxidants and helps prevent disease." That was his story and he'd stick to it.

She snorted. "Sure. Because when I order pizza I'm concerned about the nutrients. So if you get pineapple, please have them put it on the side so the juice doesn't ooze onto my half."

He quirked a brow. "Half? You're half my size and you plan on eating half the pizza?"

"Absolutely. Order a large. That way you'll be sure to get enough. And please tell me Campbell keeps you stocked up with excellent red wine."

"On it." He crossed the to the wine fridge in the kitchen area of the open plan great room. "And yeah, Campbell does––how about a Rhone blend from Paso?"

"That sounds fabulous. We deserve a treat after this afternoon. I still cannot believe that woman hijacked my boots." Lucy snickered.

He grinned at the sound of her larger-than-life laugh. "We do. Like I said, I'm not sure how you handle these type of people all the time. Do you mind opening the wine while I order dinner and feed Frank?"

She popped up from the couch, Frank at her side. "Absolutely. Where's the corkscrew?"

Cam pointed toward the drawer next to his stainless-steel stove and buried his face in his phone, not trusting his expression. Somehow it was if all the years had melted away. He and Lucy fell into a natural rhythm, hanging on a Friday night like they had for years. No tension. No stress. Familiar and new at the same time. Warmth filled his chest.

The first few years without Lucy had been the worst. Granted, he'd been consumed with punishing training and his first deployment. But at night, even when he'd collapse into his bunk completely spent, flashes of her bright smile or the expression she made when she came pierced his heart and had him tossing and turning until dawn.

Over the years and the distance, the memories faded but

they'd never disappeared. And now, with her in his home, a long dormant seed was unfurling within him. Simply spending time with her again felt like they hadn't been separated for more than a decade.

Lucy's appealing citrus aroma reached him before she appeared and offered him a glass of deep red wine. "Where's Frank's food?"

Their fingers brushed, sending a flicker of heat up his arm, another reminder of how they'd never been able to keep their hands off each other. He retreated and pivoted toward the pantry. "Just ordered ours online and I'll get his now." Time to maintain some distance between them.

He stalked to the pantry, Frank on his heels. Unfamiliar feelings were battling to escape the tight vault in the back of his heart. And a certainty was pervading his system––a certainty that he'd made the biggest mistake of his life breaking up with Lucy all those years ago. What if he had left the door open, as she'd suggested?

"Can I do anything to help?" Lucy called from the kitchen. He winced––she was probably wondering what the hell was taking him so long.

"Just take your wine into the living room and find something on TV. I'll be right out." Create a wedge of space for him to pull it together so he could keep his desire for her under control.

"Oooh, I get control of the remote control. Times have changed." Her voice was bubbling with laughter.

His lips twitched––saved by her humor. So, maybe he'd been selfish with the remote back in the day. "Only because I'm taking care of the dog. Don't get any ideas." He glanced up after mixing raw dog food with kibble and presenting it to Frank, whose tongue lolled in appreciation.

"Oh, we're watching a period piece tonight, for sure. A really long one with difficult accents. Think Victorian

England, not Vikings." She brandished the remote control like a Viking ax.

He groaned but couldn't help laughing. "You'd do that to me, wouldn't you?"

"I thought you were trying to weasel your way into my good graces, right? This is a start." Her grin was cheeky.

"Alright. I'm tough. I can handle it." He forced a lightness he didn't feel into his tone. They were slowly building something new, and he needed to act like an old friend and co-worker, not some remorseful heartsick clown.

She sat on the far edge of the sofa, her legs tucked beneath her, and her beauty hit him like a punch to his gut. Like it had all the nights they'd hung out at their parents' houses in high school and his dorm room in college. Damn, he'd royally fucked up ending things the way he had. He scrubbed a hand across his face and sat on the opposite end of his enormous L-shaped couch.

She gazed at the two broad cushions separating them, her big brown eyes wide. "I don't bite. Or did you save the middle for Frank?"

On cue, the dog bounded in from the kitchen, leapt onto the couch, and rested his head on Cam's thigh. Yeah, the mutt definitely wasn't cut out to be a service dog but damned if he didn't make him smile. Plus, Frank saved him from another awkward moment with Lucy.

They both laughed and the tension softened. "My mom's friend told me not to allow him up on the furniture, but since it looks like he's home, it won't matter."

Lucy tilted her head, her shiny hair falling over one slender shoulder. "So, you've already decided he's yours? Not just a foster?"

He gave a rueful grin. "Yeah. The guy got me on day one. But I'm not telling my mom for a while though. She'll give me her 'I told you so' routine and I don't want her to know I caved so fast."

Her full pink lips curved up. "Your mom specializes in being right all the time. Don't make her wait too long though."

He lifted his glass in a toast and she tapped hers against it above Frank. "To the newest member of the Taylor family, to Frank."

Her smile faltered but she caught herself and looked down at Frank, scratching behind his ears. "He's a lucky boy."

Cam mentally kicked himself. On their walk, she'd shared how she'd expected to be the next member of the Taylor family and once again, he was an insensitive ass. She was too damn kind. Too kind for him.

"Okay, so for tonight, no discussion of work. We'll just watch some TV, have some pizza, relax, and then I'll take you home later, cool?" He could at least handle that without saying something thoughtless again, couldn't he?"

She nodded, focused her gaze on the screen, and pressed play. "Sounds perfect to me. And your TV is so big it's like being at the movies."

He sank back into the cushions and stretched his legs out in front of him. His left quadriceps was cramping again, like it did many nights. If he'd been alone, he would have removed his artificial limb once he'd settled in. Often, he'd fall asleep on the couch, and then use his cane and some one-legged maneuvers to make it to his room. But despite the ache, he wasn't about to remove his leg in front of Lucy. Hell, he hadn't taken it off in front of anybody, not even his parents or the guys.

He downed a mouthful of wine and tried to focus on the old-fashioned movie playing in front of him. One glance at the horse drawn carriages and enormous hats and his eyelids grew heavy. He was toast. Damn, no way would he be able to stay awake, not after the grueling week.

He glanced at Lucy, who was transfixed by the screen, a small smile hovering on her mouth. At least she liked it. Frank started snoring like a warthog and Cam bit the inside of his cheek to stifle his laughter. Lucy didn't seem offended by the dog's dozing off so maybe she'd cut him a break, too.

A knock on the door resolved his dilemma. He hurried to the door, paid for the pizza, and set it on the low steamer-trunk-style coffee table where Lucy had placed plates and napkins. She paused the movie and whipped open the box. His mouth watered from the steaming aroma of sauce and cheese.

"Frank, go to your bed." The dog gave him a mournful look and slinked off to his fancy dog bed next to the couch.

"Okay, that smells delicious and I'm so glad you chose to forego the pineapple. Pure pepperoni is the way to go." Lucy picked up a generous slice, bit in, and moaned. The sound shot straight through him, and every muscle stiffened.

Cam scooted to the opposite edge of the couch again. Safer that way. *Focus on the food, not the visceral memory of the sounds Lucy made when she orgasmed.*

She flipped the show back on and they each polished off a few slices in relative quiet. So far, so good. The sooner the ending credits flashed, the sooner he could claim exhaustion and go to bed. Alone.

When they each leaned forward to place their plates on the table, Frank leapt up in a dramatic attempt to snag the pizza. The dog bumped Lucy and she fell against Cam. His breath lodged in his throat. Lucy's hands landed on his shoulders, and she lifted her wide eyes to his, her pink lips parted.

Cam's resistance dissolved. *Fuck it.* He lowered his mouth and captured hers in a kiss. Lucy's fingers dove into his hair and her long nails dug into his scalp, shooting flames straight down his spine. He growled, slid his hands down her back, and scooped her up and settled her onto his lap. She rocked her hips against him, and he went stone hard.

His self-control shattered. He captured Lucy's delicate face in his hands, and plundered her tempting mouth, deep and hot and possessive. He shifted to nibble along her jawline to the sensitive flesh beneath the shell of her ear. Her head dropped to the side, allowing him access to her satiny soft skin. She moaned and pressed her palms against his chest, where his heart raced like a jackhammer beneath her touch.

Her fingers leisurely trailed over his pecs, down his abdomen and teased the button of his jeans. His cock strained against the fabric, and he used his teeth on the tender spot where her neck met her collarbone.

"Cam, oh god." Her voice was a low purr.

Yeah, the memory of their bodies hadn't faded. He jolted. What the hell were they doing. He slid his hands to clasp her hips and pressed her away to create a sliver of space between them.

She wove her arms around her neck and pulled his mouth back to hers. "Don't stop kissing me."

"You make it really hard to stop." He growled against her sweet mouth before diving in again, deepening the kiss. *Just one more kiss.*

She collapsed against him, plastering her breasts against his chest, and swirled her tongue against his. Her nipples were taut and hard against him. She tasted delicious--hints of spicy wine and a sweet flavor all her own. Passion surged and he growled, his mouth claiming hers, his mind lost to anything but her.

Despite the past, despite the pain he'd caused her, despite

his scars and insecurities, she wanted him. He was a lucky bastard.

She stroked one hand beneath the hem of his shirt and caressed his bare skin, leaving a trail of fire with her fingertips. "Take it off." She pressed her open mouth to his throat and without thinking he reached for the cotton and yanked it off and tossed it somewhere.

He reclined back into the cushions and watched her looking at him. "Is this what you wanted?"

"Mmm-hmm. You're more perfect than I remembered." Her melted-chocolate eyes were hooded, her lips wet.

"You're the perfect one." Perfect for me.

Without breaking their gaze, she leaned forward and brushed her lips across the jagged scar on his shoulder. "I remember when you did this. Sneaking out of your parents' house and getting caught on the edge of the windowsill sneaking back in."

He grunted. "That night was worth it." He'd helped her climb out of her bedroom window and they'd gone down to the park and made out and watched the stars.

"But still. I hated that you got hurt." She pressed another open-mouthed kiss on the rough skin before continuing her sweet assault toward his throat.

He stiffened when she reached down and inch by inch, oh so slowly, unzipped his pants. When she palmed his rigid length through the thin layer of his boxer briefs, his back arched and he hissed through gritted teeth. "Lucy."

"You feel so good." She murmured against his neck before lifting her mouth to his once again.

He clasped her hips, her hot center burning against him. Their kiss grew wild with lips and tongue and teeth. He couldn't get enough of her. She squeezed her thighs, their hips rocked, and suddenly her weight dropped onto his left thigh. A dagger of pain bolted through him.

"Dammit." He grunted and pushed her to the side.

She tumbled onto the cushions next to him, her voice shaky. "Cam, your leg. I'm so sorry."

He leaned forward, his elbows on his knees, and dropped his head in his hands. "It's not your fault. Just give me a minute." He sucked in a few deep inhales, working to manage the shooting pain ricocheting along his leg.

He took some ragged breaths, willing the agony to subside. Damn it, he needed to be alone. "I'm going to take you home." He shifted back and zipped up his pants.

Lucy laid a hand on his shoulder. "Cameron, tell me if there's something I can do? Something I can get you?"

He avoided her gaze and pushed to his feet, his heart thundering in his chest, his legs unsteady. "I just need to be alone. I don't know what I was thinking but this was a mistake."

She exhaled loudly and rose. "It didn't feel like a mistake to me." She adjusted her clothes and smoothed back her hair; her soft mouth pressed into a firm line.

He whipped his head toward her. "We need to leave this in the past. You don't need this. I don't want to make things awkward for you at work."

"Oh please. Here you go again, telling me what I need. Is this because of your leg? Because I don't care about your injuries and your scars. You don't think everyone has them even if they might not be as apparent from the outside? We're all scarred. That's life. You can't use it as an excuse not to live your life fully. That's fear ruling and you're no coward." She pointed at him.

He ground his molars together. "I'm not a coward. I'm a realist. And the reality is we work together. This is my chance to start fresh and you said this is your dream job. Neither of us can afford to mess this up."

Her fingers curled into fists. "Bullshit. People work

together all the time--remember your friends Ryan and Jack? They are handling it just fine with Charlie and Campbell."

"Yeah, but we've got a different history and I'm too fucked up--you deserve better." *A man who could sleep through the night without nightmares, a man who hadn't broken your heart.*

Lucy rolled her eyes. "Oh please. We were always great together and you know it. And it's not like I'm perfect. I didn't tell you this before, but I've been engaged three times. I broke them off every single time because none of them were you."

He reared back--he couldn't have heard her correctly. "Three times? When? Who?"

She shook her head. "It doesn't matter who or when. What matters is that I refuse to give up on life. At least I'm willing to try and make mistakes. I do want to get married and have a family--like your parents. You saying you're too scarred? Seriously? More like scared. We've had the same lessons, you and me, with my cancer and your experience overseas. Life is short. And I'm out of here."

"Wait, let me get my keys." She'd been engaged to three different men? What the actual hell?

She held up one delicate hand. "I'm calling an Uber. I'm furious with you right now and I don't want to say something I regret."

Like dropping the bombshell that she'd had three fiancés and calling him a coward weren't enough? She'd actually used a curse word, so no question she was royally pissed.

"Please let me take you. You don't have to talk to me." Frank was leaning against him, offering comfort. Hell, he didn't even deserve that from the dog.

She'd already marched to pull her phone out of her purse and was punching in the ride request. "No, I don't have to talk to you. Or see you either. I need to cool off. So just go away until the car arrives."

"Lucy." His shoulders sagged and the pizza sat like a boulder in his belly.

She turned her back, stuffed her arms into her coat, and strode to the front door. She whipped it open and pulled it closed behind her with a quiet click.

"Damn it." How had tonight turned into such a disaster? He picked up the pizza box and plates and carried them to the kitchen, Frank on his heels. He tossed everything onto the counter and slammed both hands down on the kitchen island.

He gripped the smooth granite until his knuckles turned white, but he couldn't stem the erratic thump, thump, thump of his heart or the sweat drenching the back of his shirt. The panic was rising in his body, threatening to consume him-- he had to stop it.

Push-ups--he'd knock out one hundred push-ups and end the feelings bubbling inside him. He dropped to the tile floor, squeezed his eyes shut and lowered his chest to the floor and wrenched it back up. Down, up. Down, up. Down, up. Behind his eyelids, the nightmare reel started rolling.

He peered over the edge of the low stone fence, his eyes scanning for the enemy, searching for danger. Beside him, Hawkins crouched behind the corner of the crumbling building, breathing as quietly as possible. The way they'd been trained. Play possum. Act invisible and maybe you were.

Hawkins tapped him and pointed, signaling he was taking the patrol around the seemingly deserted village square. Debris from demolished buildings created mounds of concrete and wood, like an obstacle course in hell. Even through his bulletproof clothing and helmet, the stench of rotten garbage or worse filled the air.

It was a routine check, so he figured he'd accompany his soldier. They rose silently and remained in the shadows, close to the walls that still stood. Silence reigned; the only sound was his own breath. He and Hawkins reached the far edge of the square when a staccato noise echoed just past the edge of the path.

Suddenly, the world exploded, flames and stones and dirt filling the air. He dropped to the earth, but the burning blast surrounded him, pungent smoke enveloping him. His eardrums rang, and he gulped for oxygen, his mouth desert dry. A moment later, an eerie quiet replaced the noise.

He shook his head, working to clear the ringing in his ears and looked around for Hawkins. Thick smoke billowed around him but he managed to discern a body a few feet away. He rolled to the side and tried to stand. The moment he tried to put weight on his left leg, agony seared through him and he screamed.

He'd been hit. Had Hawkins? Is that why he wasn't moving?

He half-dragged, half-crawled to check on his guy. In the darkness, all he could discern was a silhouette. He reached out for a shoulder to check how bad it was.

Bile filled his throat. Hawkins was basically split into pieces, one arm gone, his face a bloody mess, and an enormous hole in his chest.

He screamed again, no sound coming out.

His eyes flew open, and he dropped to his belly on the hard, cold floor. His breath came in ragged pants and sweat poured down his face. Fucking flashbacks hit him when he allowed the stress to overtake him. Usually, a tough workout kept them at bay, but he hadn't caught it in time.

Frank threw himself down next to him and licked his face. Cam's lips curved up and he sighed out a cleansing breath. Maybe having a therapy dog around wasn't a burden after all. He scratched behind the animal's velvety ears.

Canine companion or not––no way would he be getting any sleep tonight. Even though he wasn't good enough for Lucy, picturing her engaged to anyone else pierced his heart like a knife.

CHAPTER 10

*L*ucy changed her outfit for the third and final time, satisfied the sweater covered in scarlet poppies and faded boyfriend jeans looked cheerful and cute. The last time she'd seen Mrs. T, she'd been a blubbering mess, so it was important she looked happy and confident. And since that was the exact opposite of how she'd been feeling since Friday night, it was important, at least on the surface, she appeared to have herself together.

She'd managed to avoid Cam at Cypress Coast Ranch. But over the last few days, in between bouts of intensive discussions with caterers, local musicians and DJs, florists, and every other potential business contact imaginable, she'd obsessed about every moment from Friday night. Kissing him again had felt like coming home——not exactly conducive to a platonic work relationship.

No question their chemistry remained explosive. The steamy make-out session had basically caused heat to pool in her belly and something to tighten in her heart. The scene after she'd accidentally landed on his leg. The angry words that still hung in the air between them. The heartbreaking revelation he might truly believe he didn't deserve love or was simply too scared to be vulnerable?

She buttoned her navy wool peacoat, wrapped her favorite fluffy white scarf around her neck, and hurried to her car. Christine Taylor was always early, and Lucy wouldn't make her wait. After all, she had ten more minutes solo in the car to brood about Cam. To grieve for him and his experience in war. Grieve for his losses. Grieve for their lost years. He'd shouldered such a burden alone. Her heart ached for him.

The parking gods were with her, and she scored a space close to Plumes, the oldest coffee house in Monterey. She exited her car and the freezing wind battered her. If anything, the breeze had picked up, the cold damp air a peppering of tiny needles along her skin. Not exactly appealing outdoor weather. She burrowed her face into her scarf and sped along the sidewalk to the coffee shop's entrance.

When she opened the door, she spotted Mrs. Taylor at one of the small round café tables by the windows. The delicious aroma of freshly ground beans filled her senses and she sniffed appreciatively. Plumes always smelled like heaven.

Cam's mom rose and hurried toward her, with a broad smile on her lovely face, and her arms spread wide. "Come here, beautiful girl. It's so wonderful to see you again."

They hugged in the middle of the cozy restaurant and Lucy's eyes closed with joy. How she'd missed Mrs. T's bear hugs. For a willowy fine-boned woman, the woman could squeeze tight. "It's great to see you, too."

She stepped back and returned Mrs. T's smile. "And you haven't aged a day, how is that possible?" Cam's mom was a pretty woman, with her son's unusually pale blue eyes and fine features.

Mrs. T fluttered her eyelashes and caught Lucy's hands in

hers. "Flattery will get you everywhere, sweetie. But I was already planning on treating you to breakfast."

"I'm treating. Remember, I'm your new wedding planner and it's a business expense." She winked. Technically, they were discussing the renewal of the Taylors' wedding vows at Cypress Coast Ranch. A conversation about Cam didn't change that.

"I insist. You can get it next time. I'm just so thrilled to see you looking so grown-up and beautiful. Let's order at the counter and then we can sit and catch up." Mrs. T wrapped one arm around her back and herded her toward where the barista stood.

Lucy ordered her favorite giant oat milk latte and the breakfast sandwich and Mrs. T followed suit.

Once they'd returned to their table, Mrs. T reached across and caught one of her hands and squeezed tight. "I'm still pinching myself that you're really here and working with Cam. It feels like fate, doesn't it?"

Lucy ran her tongue around her teeth. How much did she want to share with Cam's mom? From the first time they'd met when she was fourteen years old, they'd formed a special bond, even though they'd lost touch. It was boggy ground.

"It's definitely a coincidence. And a lucky one since I'm reconnecting with you again." She shrugged and smiled.

Mrs. T's brow furrowed. "Did you consider changing your mind once you learned you'd be working with Cam?"

Lucy exhaled. "I may have panicked but Joy talked me off the ledge. Reminded me it's been thirteen years and that I'd had serious relationships since Cam." Three failed engagements, like some type of pop star.

"And it would be silly to turn down your dream job because you'd once dated the boss." Mrs. T nodded.

Once dated? If only it were that straightforward. "Well, when you put it like that, sure. I mean, I've been working my whole career toward a position of this scale."

Mrs. T's lips curved up. "You know I'm a big believer in things happening for a reason. We may not know why at the time, but at some point, it becomes clear. You and Cam were so in love and although you broke up years ago, here you are back together."

Lucy shifted in her seat. "We're not back together."

"I mean, you're back in the same town and working for the same company. I know there's a lot of pain on both sides. Just so you know, we were devastated to lose you in our lives. Clyde and I love you like a daughter and I wish I'd done a better job staying in touch with you, despite it all." Mrs. T patted her hand.

Warmth filled her. "Me too. I felt a little awkward and figured it was better that way. Now I see that was a mistake. I've missed you, too."

The Taylors had been her extended family and she hadn't been particularly close to her own parents. Now they lived in nearby Pacific Grove, Lucy would make an effort to spend time with them––regardless of how things went with Cameron.

The barista called out Lucy's name and she rose to fetch their breakfast tray.

Mrs. T sniffed appreciatively, "Oh, everything smells delicious. What a lovely treat, having breakfast out on a Tuesday. I don't know when I'll get used to this retiree schedule."

"You two are so young to be retired but bravo. What are you doing now?" Lucy bit into her hearty egg and avocado sandwich, savoring the explosion of flavors in her mouth.

"Well, we bought a true fixer-upper, so we're working on some of the renovations ourselves and have ideas for part-time gigs to stay busy. We just moved so the house is consuming most of our time."

Mrs. T filled her in about Clyde's joy demolishing walls and just how many shades of pearl gray actually existed. Their conversation flowed like the intervening years had disappeared, like shrugging on a cozy old sweater. Just like she and Cam had settled into their old camaraderie over pizza and T.V.

And enough of the Cam channel running amok in her brain. She squared her shoulders. "Okay, let's move on to your vow renewal. I just love this idea. How many years have you two been married?"

"Well, we eloped when we were very young and never actually had a real wedding. It will be forty years, if you can believe it." Mrs. T sipped her steaming drink.

Lucy's gasped and her eyes widened. "Forty years. That's incredible and so inspiring. Congratulations."

Mrs. T flashed a self-deprecating grin. "I'd never advise anyone to get married so young, but for us, it worked out perfectly. Everyone's different."

Different was one word for it--like the three unmarried Taylor children and Lucy's three failed engagements. But this wasn't about her. "So, do you want a full-scale wedding or more of a vow renewal ceremony? Tons of guests or just close family and friends?"

Mrs. T contemplated for a moment. "Well, I don't think we need bridesmaids at this point and I'm definitely not wearing a white dress, but we'd like it to be festive. A big celebration. It's also a turning point in our lives--moving, retiring, starting fresh."

"I love it. You know the resort opens in May and we're solidly booked through next summer, which is incredible. If you're willing to do it on a weekday, I know we can make it work. But we did leave some leeway for dates and maybe we have it before the resort opens. I'd suggest in the gardens because they're gorgeous and you have the ocean view without too much of the salt spray."

"Can we arrange for Clyde and me to come over and check them out? We don't mind the construction. We'll just need to make sure Clyde doesn't try to join the crew." A broad smile lit up Mrs. T's face.

Lucy grinned. "Of course, I'll make sure to hide the hard hats. I'm surprised Cam hasn't had you over?"

Mrs. T's brows drew together. "Well, Cam still seems to think we moved down here because we thought he needed coddling. Has he told you about his injury yet, Lucy?"

She gave another quick nod. "He did. I'm so sad for him that he lost one of his soldiers, along with losing his lower leg."

"You know more than most people about holding scars on the inside. His leg is a dramatic loss, but he did an excellent rehabilitation program in Texas. He gets around without any assistance. I just worry about the rest." Mrs. T sighed.

"You mean the emotional and mental ramifications?" Lucy's throat constricted.

"Yes, the PTSD from losing some of his soldiers, from spending all that time in an active war zone. So, being closer to him makes Clyde and me feel better in many ways. We missed him so much." Her eyes filled.

You and me both. "I know all he ever wanted was a successful military career. Is there a reason he didn't finish his commission? I know there are other amputees who stay on Active duty."

Mrs. T pursed her lips. "He could have. They wanted him to stay but I think his heart wasn't in it any longer. Not after all the losses and not with the possibility he couldn't do what he'd been trained to do, in the way he did it before. I'm not sure if he's processed it all yet.

I'm just so glad the guys followed through on their hotel

chain idea. It gives him purpose and now he's building and creating something new, instead of being on the offensive or defensive all the time."

Time to lighten it up. "That's a great point. I can't believe they actually did it. I'll never forget when they came back from their ROTC session that summer in college. All the guys, especially Jack and Cam, couldn't stop complaining about where they had to camp. I think it's wonderful and the first two properties are doing great so far."

Mrs. T's blue eyes twinkled. "Right? My son now focused on 5-Star luxury. Who would have ever thought? I'm proud of them."

"I feel lucky to be a part of the whole group and this hotel. I want to contribute to making Cypress Coast Ranch a huge success." If she could keep her heart protected around Cam. She caught her lower lip between her teeth.

Mrs. T patted her arm. "I've no doubt you will. Okay, I know you've got plenty of work to do but before we go, I want to invite you over for Sunday dinner next weekend."

"Sunday dinner?" The Taylors' weekly family dinner had always been a cheerful, fun evening. But the key word was family--and she and Cam were no longer a couple. "Are you sure I won't be imposing?"

"Impose? Don't be ridiculous. It's my house and despite the renovations, I have a working kitchen for now and the same dining room table you'll remember. Jack and Campbell are coming up for the weekend and I know they'd love to see you. Have you seen them since you accepted the job?"

Lucy's lips curved up. "I haven't. And I just love they're engaged. Remember how Campbell used to watch him with googly eyes whenever Cam brought him home from SDSU for the holidays?"

Mrs. T grinned. "I know--my sweet tomboy had a major wake-up call. And they're just perfect for each other. Once they started working together, Jack realized what Campbell knew all along."

"It's definitely like a reunion." At least with Jack and Campbell.

Mrs. T waved a hand. "So, you'll come to dinner, and we'll all catch up."

It was futile to argue with Mrs. T when she'd made up her mind. "Okay, I'd love to come. Can I bring something? Dessert? Wine?"

"Just your beautiful self at six p.m. sharp. Campbell always insists on bringing the wine and I was planning to make my strawberry pie because Jack's dropped about twenty hints for it."

Lucy beamed. "Jack's famous sweet tooth hasn't changed, I guess. Well, just text me your address and I'll be there. In the meanwhile, I'll be in touch to schedule a tour for you and Mr. T and share some potential dates for your ceremony."

"Wonderful. It's going to be a great evening." Mrs. T rose. "You ready to brave that air? I thought San Francisco was chilly but Monterey weather doesn't mess around."

Lucy stood and donned her coat. "You aren't kidding. But I love it here."

Even though nothing was simple now that Cam was back in her life.

CHAPTER 11

*L*ucy hesitated outside the quaint wood and glass front door of the Taylors' new Pacific Grove cottage. Cars filled the narrow driveway, including Cam's jeep, so she was the last to arrive for Sunday dinner. Campbell had texted her earlier to let her know Austin and Lucas were in town and were also joining them. All the Hotel Kings were in attendance, except for Ryan.

Talk about a reunion. She hadn't seen any of the tight-knit crew since college. Uncharacteristic nerves skittered down her spine. She had no reason to be anxious––they'd always gotten along but now she was working for them, instead of simply being Cam's long-distance girlfriend.

And she was exhausted because her emotions were jumbled after the last few weeks. Between their hot make-out session and its aftermath, she worried she and Cam wouldn't be able to establish a truce. Sleep had been elusive.

The door whipped open, and a stunning blonde stood framed in the doorway. "Lucy, it *is* you." Campbell promptly grabbed her into a bear hug.

Lucy's nerves evaporated and delight filled her. She hugged Cam's little sister. "It's been way too long."

Campbell stepped back but kept her hands on Lucy's shoulders, her arctic blue eyes, so like her brother's, were solemn. "I'm so sorry I was terrible at staying in touch. Can you forgive me?"

Emotion choked her. "Oh my gosh, Campbell, there's nothing to forgive. I should have reached out."

Campbell's lips turned down. "Oh no, after Cam's idiot move, I should have. And then we were both away at different universities. But now here we are. Working together for the same company. It's fantastic. I'm so happy you're here and so are my parents."

And an obvious omission of her big brother's feelings. "It's surprising, for sure. But I'm really happy too. And I want to hear all about how your childhood crush is now your husband-to-be. You and Jack––like you always dreamed."

Campbell's cheeks pinkened. "It's a funny story but we've got plenty of time to catch up. Let's go inside."

She followed Campbell into a charming foyer. A row of whimsical brass elephant coat hooks lined one wall and Lucy hung up her puffer jacket. They strolled down the pearl-gray hallway, filled with echoes of chatter and laughter. Another hit of nerves assaulted her, but she swallowed them down. She adored these people and they adored her.

Well, everyone but Cam––those feelings were a little more complex.

They reached a wide arched doorway and stepped into a 1970s time warp of a kitchen. Pea green and orange striped wallpaper covered the walls, and the cabinets were painted a matching shade of green. The aroma of Mrs. T's famous pot roast filled the air, and she and Mr. T stood near a monstrous mustard-colored stove on the far wall of the room.

Austin Michaels, Ryan's baby brother, a tall rangy man with shaggy dark hair, stood next to them, chopping vegetables on a wooden cutting board. Jack and Lucas lounged against the counter, looking like two hot guys from a beer commercial, each sipping bottles of microbrew. Cam wasn't in the room.

Mrs. T hadn't been kidding when she had referred to the cottage as a fixer upper. The updated foyer was gorgeous, but the kitchen was straight out of *That 70s Show*.

"Look who's here. Our very own Lucy Goodwin," Campbell announced.

Mr. T, wearing a cheerful red apron proclaiming him the Master Chef, crossed the room and enveloped her in a classic Taylor family hug. "Lucy, it's so great to see you again."

She relaxed into his embrace, at home at once. The Taylors were master huggers. Even Cam.

Lucy stepped back and beamed up at him. "Thanks so much for having me."

"We're just thrilled you're in town too and working with the kids. We've missed you. And you're always part of the family." Clyde Taylor's light blue eyes crinkled at the corners when he smiled. He hadn't changed much over the last several years, except now his pale hair was more silver than gold.

Mrs. T hurried over and wrapped one arm around her shoulders. "Don't monopolize her. Now what can I get you to drink, Lucy? The boys are drinking some bitter microbrew beer they're obsessed with, but Campbell and I are enjoying a delicious Merlot."

She followed Cam's mom to the narrow taupe Formica counter where an open bottle of wine awaited. "Wine for me, thanks."

"Little Lucy's all grown up." Austin set down his knife and stepped in for a hug, with Jack and Lucas close behind.

Everyone was so welcoming, and her heart warmed at their enthusiasm and kindness. Where was Cam?

Mr. T waved an arm. "What do you think of the kitchen? One of a kind, right?"

Her lips curved up. "That's one way to describe it. What's the plan for in here?"

"Plan? What do you mean? We thought it was perfect like it is." Mr. T barked out a laugh. "Actually, the kitchen is next. We'll gut it and open the far wall to the living room and absolutely no mustard or green anywhere."

Lucy grinned. "Thank goodness. I didn't think it had the Taylor charm." Although the Taylors' bay area home had been a modest ranch, it had impeccable décor that reflected Cam's mom's coastal farmhouse style.

"Well, you've got an open invitation to Sunday dinner whenever you like so you can track the progress." Cam's dad sipped his drink.

A loud woof interrupted the boisterous conversations and Frank beelined toward her, his tail flapping like helicopter wings. He bumped against her legs and gazed up at her with adoration. Lucy scratched his dark velvet ears and checked to see if Cam would also approach her.

Nope, he remained on the far side of the room. He gave a half-wave, picked up a beer, and leaned against the counter next to the guys. Maybe he'd taken her words literally Friday night and planned to avoid her all evening. Not awkward at all.

"Okay children, move it along to the dining room. Cameron, set Frank up in the den while I take out the roast. No need to tempt him to re-enact the incident that got him fired." Mrs. T called.

"Frank got fired?" Austin snickered. "Now that's a story I need to hear."

"Apparently, he stole a Thanksgiving turkey right off the

kitchen counter and that convinced the dog trainers he was better off as a well-trained pet instead of a service dog," Cam cracked a smile and escorted Frank out of the room.

"Sounds like the perfect creature to keep you in line. All hail Frank." Jack called after his buddy and toasted the dog with his beer bottle.

"All hail Frank." Everyone shouted.

Lucy turned her head away. Cam claimed to be too screwed up now to consider being with her, but he sure was able to relax around his family and friends. Once she'd been part of his inner circle––the center actually. She resisted the urge to massage the pain in her chest. It was for the best–– how could she ever trust him not to hurt her again even if he did want to try again?

Lucy fell into step between Lucas and Austin. She knew Lucas from SDSU, and Austin was Ryan's younger brother, so she'd met him a few times too. He'd been in an alt-rock band that played at some of the college parties, even though he'd still been in high school. "So, what brings you guys up to Monterey?"

Austin smiled down at her, well everyone looked down on her because she was usually the shortest person in the room. "I'll be opening the Palm Springs Hotel and Lucas is going to run Beverly Hills. I'm overseeing the restaurant arm of all the hotels so I'm here to interview a few chefs with Cam. Plus, we all pitch in at each location so we're here to do whatever Cam needs us to do."

"I'm handling a lot of the financials, so I'll check on those and lend a hand, too. It's so wild that you're here and the wedding planner for our resort," Lucas, a dead ringer for the guy who played Jamie on *Outlander*, said with a wry grin.

She waved a hand. "I know. And the Taylors moved down here, too. All roads lead to Monterey, right?"

Jack was seated across from Campbell and patted the empty chair next to him. "You come sit next to me Lucy. We've got a lot to catch up on."

Cam was already parked at the far end of the same weathered rectangular dinner table the Taylors had in San Francisco. Distance was safer--her shoulders softened when she sat next to Jack.

"Tell me everything." She beamed at the happy-go-lucky charmer--Cam's polar opposite. Jack had been a regular fixture around the Taylor household when the guys weren't off in ROTC training.

He tapped one long finger on his square chin. "Hmm… not much. Army Reserve while busting my butt in law school, buried myself in a few law firms around the country focusing on real estate and environmental issues, went into business with my brothers from another mother, and opened Maison du Soleil."

"That's all? Aren't you forgetting the most important update?" Lucy stared at Campbell, who was whispering with Austin.

"Oh yeah, just fell madly in love with my best friend's incredible little sister." Jack's jade green eyes gleamed and his full lips curved up.

Lucy clapped her hands together. "I'm so happy for you two. And I hope you'll let me plan the wedding for you. Will you do it here in Monterey like Ryan and Charlie?"

He downed a mouthful of beer. "Campbell wants us to elope to Bordeaux sometime this year and who am I to say no?"

Jack gazed at his fiancé across the table, his light-brown skin glowing. Oh, to be that madly in love. Her gaze fell on Cameron and her heart stuttered. She shook herself back to the present--they weren't together anymore.

She refocused on Jack. "That sounds incredible. I mean, maybe I can stow away in one of your suitcases and handle some details or something? I've always wanted to visit that area of France."

Jack laughed. "You're still tiny enough to sneak in but I think we'll do it solo. Mrs. T would kill us if we didn't celebrate here, so we'll probably have a casual party when we return. Your turn. Spill it--work, love life, the scoop."

She cleared her throat, picked up her wine, and took a healthy gulp. "I love being a wedding planner and although I excel at creating the perfect day for other people, I'm totally, completely single at the moment." And probably single forever since the man who made her heart skip a beat was the man who she couldn't risk opening her heart to again.

Austin piped in. "Single at the moment? Careful Lucy, these people are determined there will be an engagement at every new hotel opening. You could be next." He pointed his beer bottle at her.

Campbell smacked Austin's shoulder. "Would you be quiet, Austin--just because you're allergic to relationships doesn't mean everyone else is."

Lucy gazed up and Cam's pale eyes burned into her, his jaw tight. Her stomach flip-flopped. Did Austin and the guys assume she and Cam were casual and fine and light years away from when they were a couple? *If only.*

"I, for one, can't believe Lucy's still single. Young men today must be fools." Mr. T said as he and Mrs. T appeared bearing a platter with her world-famous roast, garnished with potatoes and carrots.

Heat rose in Lucy's cheeks. "Dinner looks incredible. I'm starving." Perfect timing. Thank god for the interruption-- no need to stoke the simmering tension between her and Cam.

They passed the steaming dishes around the table, serving family style. The Taylor Sunday dinners were full of laughter and multiple conversations going on at once, often one atop the other and Lucy relaxed.

Austin was regaling the group with a spot-on imitation of a snooty New York City chef who, when asked if he'd be interested in opening the Palm Springs hotel's restaurant, had claimed he'd rather work in New Jersey than the "god-forsaken sand pit" in Southern California. Apparently, the only place in California he'd deign to cook would be Beverly Hills.

Lucas added, "No way am I putting up with that attitude at my place. Let's hope the meetings with the candidates for Cypress Coast Ranch are a little more down to earth."

Campbell burst into laughter. "I hate to break it to you, Lucas, but down-to-earth and potential Michelin Star chefs aren't two terms often used together. Although, there are some great chefs who are personable. As long as you love their food."

"I nominate Mrs. T as chef for whichever restaurant she wants. This roast is the best I've ever had," Jack said and brandished his beer bottle.

Lucy lifted her glass. "I second the motion."

Mrs. T's blue eyes sparkled. "Oh Jack, you're already getting seconds and I made your favorite dessert, so you stop. I'm retired so if you want my cooking, you'll have to come up on Sundays to get it."

In the midst of the boisterous group, Cam quietly focused on his plate. Not that he'd ever been a talkative guy, but tonight he was almost sullen. Had Austin's comments hit too close to home? Or was he more withdrawn because she was there?

∽

Usually nothing could prevent Cam from savoring his mom's excellent cooking, but tonight every bite turned to sawdust in his mouth. Did his family and friends really think he and Lucy were unaffected by their casual comments about her being single?

Not that anyone had a clue they had kissed and likely would have slept together if his leg hadn't interrupted their session on his couch. And Lucy obviously hadn't shared her history of broken engagements.

Lucy seemed fine but he'd seen her subtle wince at Austin's light-hearted comment. Damn it, he'd sat as far away from her as possible but remained laser focused on her every expression. He couldn't help himself.

"You know we'll come up every weekend we can." Campbell smiled at their parents. "It is really great to have you guys closer."

Thank god his sister and Jack were engaged and could distract his parents' attention from him.

"So Lucy, Christine told me you'd worked in Kauai for a year? How was that?" Mr. T asked.

Kauai? Is that where she'd met one of her fiancés? His fingers tightened on his fork.

"Kauai is like stepping into a Van Gogh painting, the colors are richer and more vibrant, the air is softer, the ocean even feels softer. I worked for one of the big resorts, but it's a small community and I got a little bit of island fever. So here I am." Lucy's wide smile lit up her face.

"Charlie mentioned the same thing about the Turks and Caicos. She and Ryan both wanted to be back on the mainland eventually, too," Austin said.

Cam's heart ached as the cheerful meal progressed, so reminiscent of the days he and Lucy were a couple. Seeing her so easily fit in as part of his family was a visceral reminder of how he'd screwed things up. Despite what he'd told her the other night, he wanted her closer, not further away.

His gut clenched as the realization slammed into him, like floodlights flipping on. He'd screwed up and now he had a chance for a fresh start with Lucy if he could convince her to trust him. She might be wary of mixing business with pleasure, but they belonged together. How could he show her?

"Cam and Lucy, will you help me clear the dishes and bring in the dessert?" Mrs. T rose from the table.

"Of course." Lucy licked her lips and every muscle in Cam's body leapt to attention.

Together, they headed into the kitchen and Cam was careful to maintain his distance from Lucy. No need to get close and catch her fresh lemony scent, not when he didn't have a plan to ask her for a second chance yet. His system was already in overdrive seeing her with his family this way, recognizing all the time he'd wasted.

"Just put the dishes in the sink and then Cam, you can carry out the pie and Lucy take the plates, please. And Cameron, are you planning on sulking all night or are you going to participate in the evening with the rest of us?" Mrs. T turned and folded her arms across her chest.

Cam sputtered. "I'm not sulking. It's just hard to get a word in edgewise with everyone talking at once. Geez, Mom." Had he been that obvious?

She raised an eyebrow and swung her gaze to Lucy. "What do you think, Lucy?"

Lucy's chocolate brown eyes widened. "Um, I hadn't noticed. The conversations are lively."

Mrs. T's eyes narrowed. "Still covering for him, I see. You don't have to do that anymore. At least not when you're off the clock."

"Hey," Cam said with a frown. Whose side was his mom on?

"He's quiet with me these days, so I honestly didn't notice a difference." Lucy shrugged a shoulder, her usually expressive face impassive.

He grimaced. "I'm standing right here."

"I'll take the dessert in before Jack starts protesting." Lucy picked up the pie, pivoted, and escaped into the dining room.

Mrs. T closed her eyes for a moment and stepped in to hug Cam. "I'm sorry. It's hard seeing you two together but not together."

Cam's breath caught. "It's hard for me too, Mom."

Mrs. T stepped back and looked up at him, her expression somber. "You two still care for each other. I can see it. Are you going to try to win her back?"

Cam exhaled an unsteady breath. "I want to. Seeing her with our family tonight just hammered it home that I still love her. But I know the job is important to her and working together really complicates things. Plus, I'm not sure if she'd give me another chance, not after how I handled everything."

She stroked a hand over his hair, like she had when he was a little boy. "You did the best you could at the time. You're both older and more experienced now. And you've always done whatever you set your mind to."

"Hey, we need plates out here or Jack's threatening to start eating the pie off the platter," Austin bellowed from the other room.

Austin's obnoxiousness lifted the seriousness of the moment. "Thanks, Mom."

"But we better take in the plates or Jack will ruin that dessert." Her lips twitched.

Cam nodded, encouraged from his mom's unwavering belief in him. "You know he would, too."

His mom linked her arm through his and together they returned to the dining room. After the evening ended, he could begin strategizing a plan to win Lucy back. She still had feelings for him, which meant victory would be his, right?

CHAPTER 12

*B*efore entering his office, Cam took a steadying breath to shake off yet another sleepless night. Last night's insomnia wasn't courtesy of Afghanistan nightmares but due to the Lucy dilemma. Obviously, them working together wasn't going to be simple. And Cypress Coast Ranch was his opportunity to build a new life after losing the one he'd planned, so he couldn't screw it up. And he wouldn't screw up things with Lucy again.

Call it fate or coincidence, it didn't matter. He had a second chance at life after surviving a near death experience. How many people got to create an amazing company with their best friends? How many people got a second chance with their first love? In his case, his only love?

Since he'd returned from war and the intensive year of therapy in San Antonio, he knew he hadn't been easy to be around. Since he'd returned, he hadn't been able to confide in or explain how he was feeling to anyone, even the guys. He couldn't jeopardize their silent support and easy acceptance of his moods. No, he'd show them he could kick ass at this new gig, even if he was mostly winging it.

And he needed to show Lucy she could trust him not to hurt her again.

Work first. Poker face intact, he strode into his office's open doorway in the main lodge, where Lucas, Jack, and Austin lounged in the chairs across from his desk, debating which team would head to the Super Bowl. Typical.

Jack glanced down at his watch, looked up and smirked. "There he is. Nice of you to join us today. We've been waiting for hours. Thought you needed help with that permitting issue?"

Cam rolled his eyes. "Hours? It's 8:05."

"Not like you to be late. But we've only been here for about fifteen. We wanted to beat you in." Lucas winked.

"Sorry. And thanks for coming up. Yeah, the guy at County is suddenly claiming they won't grant some routine permits around the Certificate of Occupancy, so guests wouldn't be able to stay in the rooms." He crossed to the other side of his desk and sank into the comfortable chair he'd splurged on. "Didn't we have to jump through some extra hoops in La Jolla? We can't have a delay in the opening."

Crisis mode in the military wasn't too different than in civilian life. Both seemed to have a mountain of red tape. Although he had only months of hotel management training compared to his lifetime in the Army. Thank god he had the whole crew to navigate through it all. He couldn't let down the team or himself for that matter.

He powered on the screen and pulled up the day's calendar. "In terms of the schedule and confirming we're on track with everything else. Austin, your interviews aren't until this afternoon. Did you need me to sit in on those with you?" Please god no.

Austin shook his head. "Nah. It would be a waste of your time, especially with the Certificate of Occupancy issue. If one of these chefs seems like a good fit, I do want final approval from you though. You'll be the one dealing with them on the daily. I'll text you, cool?"

"Perfect. Okay then this morning, I definitely need your help and Jack's legal expertise. Where is Campbell? We need some numbers on corporate groups and potential impacts if we are forced to reschedule any of them."

"She and Lucy are down at the beach discussing some logistics for a few of our early events but they should be up here soon. Does Lucy know?"

Lucas quirked a ginger eyebrow. "Yeah, what does Lucy think?"

Cam stiffened. "What do you mean?"

"What does Lucy think about having to tell clients that they may need to have their weddings at a different venue or move their dates forward? What did you think I meant?" Lucas waved one hand.

Austin narrowed his eyes. "What's going on with you and Lucy? Last night it seemed like things were tense between you guys. Has it been weird seeing her again?"

Cam ran his tongue around his teeth. No secret he'd been quiet last night but the last thing he needed was the guys getting involved. "It was a shock, yeah. But we're figuring it out."

"Figuring it out? You barely even looked at her last night," Lucas said.

Jack pointed at him. "The single dumbest thing you ever did was dumping that woman––she is one of a kind. And she's single."

"And she's drop-dead gorgeous. She's single, huh?" Austin rubbed his jaw.

"Yeah, she's single." He glared at Austin. Not that the guy was interested in relationships.

"That's surprising. Hell, I can't believe you let her go," Lucas said, pushing his wire-rimmed glasses up.

Austin nodded and pointed at Cam. "If I lived closer--"

Cam held up both hands. "If you lived closer, you'd treat her like a sister. Now can we get started on figuring out how to deal with that pain in the ass who seems to make life difficult for anyone attempting to run a legitimate business? Otherwise, we're in big trouble here."

Lucas groaned. "Yeah, we've got to ensure that the Certificate of Occupancy is granted. Charlie's the one who charmed that woman in La Jolla, but she's slammed right now. I think Jack should make the call--he's the smooth talker."

"You make it sound like that's a bad thing." Jack flashed a grin. "I'm happy to do it but I need to see more details. And we need to discuss contingencies."

"Contingencies for what?" Campbell entered the office.

Lucy stood at her side, looking fresh and sexy with her windblown hair and a pink flush staining her high cheekbones. Her enormous dark eyes sparkled but she avoided looking at him. Something tugged in Cam's chest. *She* didn't appear to have lost any sleep last night.

"Hi beautiful, we've got some delays and permitting problems, so we need to brief Lucy and I'm going to make a few calls now to see the extent of it," Jack said.

"Delays? Will they impact the opening schedule?" A crease formed between Lucy's dark brows.

"If we don't get them resolved, they could because we couldn't have guests occupy the rooms. We're going to do everything to expedite the process and get it on track," Cam said, sounding more confident than he felt.

"Oh no, we're fully booked starting the week after opening--this could be a disaster. What can I do to help?" Lucy sauntered closer.

Damn, her legs looked incredible in the knee-length pencil skirt she wore with some high-heeled booties. Cam gritted his teeth--and this was part of the challenge of working with Lucy. Where were those practical boots she'd worn with the Harringtons?

Jack rose. "Everyone hold on. I'll make a few calls first and we'll get a game plan. But start thinking about alternatives like perhaps holding the wedding here and coordinating with another hotel for the guests to stay?" He strode out of the room, cell phone to his ear.

"We don't want to refer to our competition. What if clients decided to move their whole events over? It could be a disaster." Lucy nibbled on her plump lower lip.

Despite the gravity of the situation, every muscle in Cam's body tightened. He dragged his eyes from Lucy to his computer and pulled up the County building's address. "We'll work out a strategy. We will open on time if we have to go to their offices in person. It's only about thirty minutes away."

"While we're waiting on Jack, why don't you point me to some of those ledgers you wanted me to look at? I'll start knocking those out," Lucas said, rising from the chair.

"The files are all on the main server, but I emailed you a link to the ones I'd like you to review," Cam said.

"Perfect. I'll take my laptop to the lobby and work on it there. Let me know if you need me." Lucas exited the room.

"And I'll head over to the kitchen and talk to the contractors to make sure there aren't any issues on that front." Austin stood and scrubbed his hands through his messy black hair.

"I love how well you guys work together. I'm going to come with you, Austin, because I want to see if the wine storage is up to what I requested." Campbell turned and hugged Lucy before leaving with Austin. "Don't worry, everything will work out and the weddings won't be impacted."

Lucy's mouth curved up. "I like your confidence. And if

I've got to drive over to that office myself, I will. I'm good at managing challenging personalities." Her gaze caught Cam's.

Cam frowned. Lucy had pointed out how she'd handled him, and she wasn't wrong. Most curmudgeons couldn't withstand her relentless positivity. And did she see him as that type of project?

An awkward silence filled the space between them.

"You're hired." Jack burst into the room. "Mr. Stanley Smith demands that the GM of Cypress Coast Ranch come to the offices to discuss the issue in person. So, you and Cameron need to head up to Marina now."

Lucy retreated a step. "Me and Cam? Go up there together?"

Cam's fingers dug into his thighs. "Shouldn't you be going with me, Jack? You're the real estate attorney. But I can handle a meeting by myself." Did Jack not trust him to manage it alone?

"I've got something urgent that just popped up at my hotel, so I can't go. I'm not saying you can't handle it but having Lucy along could make it a lot easier. She's the wedding planner and could underscore how detrimental a delayed opening could be. Plus, like she said, she's good at handling the tough ones. You two will be like good cop/bad cop."

Lucy shook her head. "I've got a really hectic morning."

"I already told Stanley you two would be there within the hour." Jack shrugged. "I'll be on a conference call but text me if it's urgent. Get going. You guys will be fine." With that, he pivoted and left.

Lucy frowned. "Is he always that bossy?"

"Yeah, he knows how to get things done." Cam shrugged––no use fighting it. "Are you ready to go now or do you need to reschedule anything?"

She huffed out a breath. "I can make a few calls in the car

if you don't mind driving. Let me get my bag and I'll meet you at your jeep."

Cam powered off his computer and squared his shoulders. Time to problem solve. He was an excellent tactician and he'd prove his worth with this challenge. And maybe he could use the time in his car with Lucy to cement a strategy for winning her back.

TWO HOURS LATER, Lucy slammed the passenger door, dropped her head onto the headrest, and allowed her eyes to close. Between the scene at Cam's house and dinner at the Taylors' last night, she was exhausted. Throw in being in close proximity with Cam for the last few hours and all she wanted to do was curl up on her couch with a plate of brownies and watch *Friends* re-runs.

And she still had a full afternoon of meetings, including one she'd had to reschedule after Jack's insistence she accompany Cam. Good cop/bad cop––sure. Jack's green eyes had gleamed with mischief. Was he playing matchmaker?

The driver's door clicked shut and she forced her heavy eyelids open and side-eyed Cam. Heat curled down her spine and she clasped her hands together in her lap. Why did he have to be so gorgeous? In profile, he could be stamped on a darn coin. Chiseled from bronze.

He blew out an exhale. "Well, that's one way to start a Monday. That guy was a––"

"Piece of work." She finished his sentence. Like they always used to do.

He turned to her, his lips twitching. "Exactly. It's like he gets off on making other people's lives more difficult."

She nodded. "Exactly. He must be really miserable person.

But I think we'll be able to get approval in time once we jump through twenty more hoops."

"I hope so. I've got to live up to the other hotels' openings." His golden brows drew together.

"You're doing a great job, Cameron. Especially since the hospitality business is new for you. It's just how it goes during openings. The other Hotel Kings properties were lucky to be able to open on schedule--it's not the norm in my experience." And she prayed Cypress Coast Ranch would be lucky too or she'd have some catastrophes on her hands if she had to start rescheduling or canceling weddings before they'd held a single event.

His long tanned fingers tightened on the steering wheel, and he started the ignition. "Thank you. Look, Lucy, we should discuss what happened at my house--"

Her breath caught in her throat and her belly lurched. Not today. No way was she equipped to discuss their personal life, or more like their *lack* of personal life. She'd managed to maintain her seemingly calm façade because she'd slammed her emotions in the vault. And there they needed to remain.

She held up a hand. "No. Not now. If I'm going to make it through the afternoon's appointments after this stressful morning, I cannot discuss anything personal. We need to keep it all work."

His angled his gaze toward her, his square jaw clenched. "But I--"

Annoyance flared and she folded her arms across her chest. "It's great that you want to discuss things finally, but you need to respect what I want. I had to redo an entire section of the Harrington contract again because Victoria changed her mind on a few details last night at 10 o'clock and I'm not ready to talk about anything but the hotel right now. If you don't agree, I'm going to find some music to blast until we're back."

Cam frowned. "This is ridiculous. Those women have you jumping through hoops. It's okay if this wedding doesn't work out. You shouldn't have to work overtime like this."

"I will make it work, don't worry." Lucy's jaw tightened.

"But what I'm saying is that it's okay if it doesn't. I don't like seeing them taking advantage of you like this."

Lucy flashed a tired grin. "Oh, I'm used to it. Wedding planning is not a 9 to 5 job. But yes, once in a while the clients can be frustrating. But I'm closing this deal if it kills me. And we especially need to nail it down if this permit nonsense isn't resolved."

"That's my concern. I know you're amazing at what you do, Lucy. I know you're amazing, period. But know that I don't expect you to work 24/7. And if you don't close every single deal, that's okay too." His deep raspy voice was serious.

"Look at you being all sweet. I appreciate it. Trust me, I'm fine. But I'd really like to not talk for a few minutes." His sincerity was causing her heart to gallop in her chest and her belly to flutter.

"And you call me stubborn. Fine. Pick some music. We're taking a few extra minutes to take the coast because I need to clear my mind." He pulled out of the crowded parking lot and headed toward Hwy 1.

"Fine, you're the boss. I'm already two hours behind schedule, what's another forty-five minutes." She pursed her lips, leaned forward, and fiddled with the satellite radio stations until she found a cheesy 80s station playing Bon Jovi's "Living on a Prayer." Fitting.

"You wanted to keep it to work. And I'm going to hop on the 17-Mile Drive and cruise by the Inn at Spanish Bay and the Lodge at Pebble Beach. Technically checking out the competition, right?"

She shrugged a shoulder. "Sure. They've already got most of the wedding business in the area, and it makes sense why." Part of her excitement over her role at Cypress Coast Ranch was the chance to shake up the major competitors on the peninsula.

"You'll change all that. I know we're going to be a player and you're a major part of it." He gazed at her, his crystal blue eyes warm.

Her heart softened. "Thank you. Now, I meant it. No more talking until we get back to the resort. I'm going to enjoy the music and the views."

"Sounds like a plan." He nodded and focused on the road.

She loved 17-Mile Drive and when she and Sue had first moved to Monterey, they'd taken the scenic road through Pebble Beach and the Monterey Peninsula so many times that a few of the gate guards thought they worked at one of the resorts.

Between the jaw-dropping ocean views, the sprawling mansions, and enormous forest of Monterey Cypress trees, Lucy couldn't get enough of the raw beauty. It tended to ground her and remind her that no matter what was happening in her life, places like this existed. Nothing like the power of nature to keep things in perspective. The tension in her neck and shoulders relaxed.

And for the next little while, they rode in companionable silence, the rugged cliffs and watercolor sky soothing her soul. Sharing it with Cam was bittersweet with so much up in the air between them. But right now, the quiet and the majestic surroundings reminded her that life was beautiful.

For the moment, that was enough.

CHAPTER 13

Cam loaded Frank into the front seat of his Jeep. The dog preferred riding shotgun and why not? He fastened Frank's seatbelt because otherwise the car's automatic alarm would beep incessantly, and he wasn't in the mood.

"I can't take it anymore. Can you take it anymore?" He glanced over at Frank, the dog's gaze soulful and contemplative, one ridiculous floppy ear twitching.

And here he was talking to his dog. His mom hadn't had to point out his behavior to him Sunday night. Especially in front of Lucy. Lucy's big brown eyes had always revealed her feelings, at least with him. And even though she'd quickly banked the emotion, he'd caught the flash of hurt.

But in the moment, it had all been too damn much to handle. Lucy sitting across the table, laughing with Jack, like they had back in the day. Lucy just fit in with his family and the way he'd handled their break-up had deprived her of not just their long-term relationship, but also her close connection with his family and friends. How much pain could he inflict on her? He needed to clear the air and ensure she was comfortable at work. If he could convince her to give him another chance too, he'd be a lucky bastard.

The other night's melding of the present with the past had fired something in his chest. Add in Monday's car ride and her unwillingness to allow him to apologize and he had to act. Damn it, when had he become a coward? Despite his medals for bravery and his reputation of being fearless in the face of the enemy, he'd been scared to examine his true feelings. Her resilience, her beauty, and her compassion were impossible to resist. Damn it, he wanted to see her. He needed to see her tonight and ask these questions because he couldn't handle another sleepless night. They needed some type of resolution.

One way or the other.

He flicked on the ignition and pointed the car toward Lucy's cottage.

He peeked at Frank. "Okay boy, this is what's going to happen. First, I'm going to apologize to Lucy for everything. And if she doesn't boot me out, I'm going to ask her to tell me about these ex-fiancés. Because even though I don't have a right to know, I need to know."

Frank didn't respond, which obviously was tacit agreement. Or hell, maybe making assumptions was why he was in this situation. If this week at the hotel was any indication, Lucy would not be thrilled to see him. Cam's fingers tightened on the steering wheel, and he regulated his breathing.

He parked in front of her cottage, with its lights glowing from inside. Doubt gripped him--should he text her and ask permission or show up on her doorstep? Wasn't there some saying about better to beg for forgiveness? Add it to his list.

Lucy was impulsive so maybe she'd appreciate his spontaneity.

"Come on boy, let's do this." He exited the car and led Frank to the front door. His heart hammered against his ribcage and sweat prickled along the back of his neck, despite the cool January evening. He exhaled an unsteady breath and rapped on the door.

After what felt like hours, the door opened a crack and Lucy peered up at him.

"What are you doing here?" Her dark eyes narrowed.

His gut twisted. "Will you come out and go for a ride with me and Frank? We need to talk."

Lucy shook her head, maintaining the barrier between them. "I don't think we've got much to discuss except for work, so can't it wait for the office?"

He massaged the tight cords on the back of his neck. "You wanted to discuss the past before. Please. Can I come in and apologize? Just give me fifteen minutes."

She nibbled on her lower lip. Before she could answer, Frank took matters into his own paws and shoved the door open, yipping with joy. Yeah, so maybe Frank was the best wingman ever because she couldn't resist the adorable mutt.

Lucy sighed, stepped back, and waved him inside. "Well, I guess Frank made the decision for us. Look, I'm tired and I'm irritable and I'm not in the mood for a big talk tonight, okay? I'll give you fifteen minutes."

He nodded and stepped through the doorway into her cozy home. "Thank you."

She crossed the room, sat on the couch, and clasped her hands in her lap. A glass of red wine sat on her low coffee table, but she didn't touch it nor did she offer to pour him a glass.

He sat in the navy velvet armchair across from her and Frank plopped down next to Lucy's feet and stared up at her with adoration.

She scratched Frank's ears, glanced at her watch, and gestured one artistic hand toward him. "Your time clock is running."

"I deserve that." He rubbed his palms along his jeans and met her gaze. "I'm really sorry about Sunday night. Seeing you with my family and friends again was rough and--"

A crease appeared between her brows. "You think it was rough for you? How do you think I felt? Everyone was so welcoming, and you barely spoke to me. And that's not really an apology."

"Please let me finish, okay? You were right about what you said--I was an idiot when I left for not discussing our future. I don't know if we would have decided to keep up the long-distance but not having a conversation was really immature. It's been weighing on me. And Sunday--it was a reminder of how well you fit in with my family, a reminder of how incredible we were together. And I just froze." His pulse kicked through his veins.

Her eyes widened and she tilted her head. "So you not talking to me was fear? Fear of what?"

He cleared his throat. "Fear and the realization that I made an enormous mistake and seeing how we're thirteen years forward and how things could have been, I don't know."

She drew in a sharp inhale. "You mean if we'd been a couple? If we'd been married by now and it was just another Sunday night with the family?"

He nodded. "Yeah."

She threw her hands up in the air. "And your solution was to ignore me until your mom called us into the kitchen? It doesn't sound like there's been a lot of growth from the 22-year-old who dumped me and the 35-year-old man who should know better by now."

His fingers dug into his thighs. "I'm here now to apologize. I'm trying, Lucy."

She reached for her wine and sipped. "Apology accepted. But why? So our work relationship goes smoothly? So we don't make everyone around us uncomfortable?"

He leaned forward. "Not just for work. You said something the other night at my house and I can't stop thinking about it."

"We said a lot of things the other night." Her gaze lowered, her dark lashes shadowing her cheeks.

She wasn't going to make this easy. "You said I was making excuses not to be with you. That's not how I see it."

Her gaze met his, her eyes hot. "Well, why don't you tell me how you see it then? Because it sounded to me like you're afraid to get involved with anyone because you have scars. That's a cop-out because your experiences and your losses only make you more resilient. Don't you see that?"

He exhaled an unsteady breath. "I hear what you're saying. Logically, I know what you're saying is right. And I know what you survived and how it shaped you into who you are. That's one thing––I'm still adjusting, okay? I have nightmares and have a tough time sleeping through the night; I had a panic attack after you left. I don't feel as strong as I was. So it was easier to keep you at arm's length instead of admitting it."

Her expression softened. "I'm sorry, Cam. I can't imagine what you went through and I'm not trying to make light of it. But that's only part of who you are. Not all of you and that's life, right? Can't you see that you're stronger? That you're forging a new life despite your setbacks? It takes a lot of courage to accept what you've planned is no longer an option and to switch gears. You've done that."

He squeezed his eyes closed for a moment, allowing the effect of her words to flow through him like a stream of cool water soothing his jagged nerves. He understood what she was saying but damn if it was simple to internalize it. To own it. "Maybe."

"It explains how you acted on that Friday night, but not at your parents' house. Why did you come here now? Why couldn't you wait until I told you I was ready?"

Now or never. "Two things. First, you said it didn't feel like a mistake."

She licked her lips. "Kissing you didn't feel like a mistake. Either time. What's the second question?"

He shifted in the chair, every muscle in his body leaping to attention. "You said you'd been engaged three times and broken each one off because none of them were me. I guess I haven't been able to stop thinking about how you fell in love three times and agreed to marry three guys. I'm wondering if you still have feelings for any of them?"

She grabbed her wine and took a long sip before answering. "Before I answer this question, is that a note of judgment in there for me moving on with my life after you disappeared?"

"Not judgment but I can't help but wonder why you didn't end up marrying one of them. And if I'm honest, I hate thinking of you in love with anyone else." His jaw clenched.

"You haven't been in love in the last thirteen years? Seriously?" She tilted her head, one dark brow arched.

He shook his head. "No. I told you my priority was the Army. It always came first. After ending things with you, I didn't want to go through that kind of pain again. I had a few girlfriends over the years but I was up front that it wouldn't ever be serious."

And no woman he'd met had ever measured up to Lucy. He'd liked some women, cared about them, but his heart had never been in any danger. And it stung to know she'd shared hers with someone else, even though it was his own damn fault.

She looked down at her hands. "Huh. Well, I don't really know what you want me to say. My career is important, and

I love it, but personal relationships are too. I've always known I want to have a life partner, my ride or die. I want it all."

Something tugged in his chest. "And you thought these other guys could be your ride or die?"

Lucy rose from the couch and strode over to the small kitchen island. She was wearing a pair of fluffy bunny ear slippers, like the ones she'd favored as a teenager. His lips twitched, even amid the serious conversation. How had he ever let her go?

She stood with her back to him, posture rigid, and refilled her wine glass. "It looks like we're talking for more than fifteen minutes. Do you want something to drink?"

That had to be a good sign, right? He didn't want to leave until he'd shown her he was sorry and find out if they could leave the past behind. "A glass of water would be great. And maybe some for Frank?" The dog's tail thumped on the floor.

She gazed back over her shoulder. "Of course. Still no ice for you?" When he nodded, pleased she remembered his preference, she filled a large glass from the filtered water in her fridge and a bowl for Frank.

Once she'd set them down, she returned to the sofa, and met his gaze. "Okay, I'll give you the overview. For a few years after you left, I didn't get serious about anyone. I couldn't. But as time went on and I was living my life, I ended up meeting someone, got serious, then ended it. Repeat that two more times. Different guys, different issues, different feelings. And yes, I did love all of them, in different ways. If I look back now and really consider it, I don't think I was ever truly 'in love' with any of them. Not enough to marry them anyway."

He'd asked but damn, to hear her say she'd loved other guys. And visuals of her with other men, not just physically but emotionally, was like a knife to his heart. "But they obviously all were in love with you if they proposed. And men don't usually propose unless they think the woman will say yes, right?" Or at least that's what he figured.

She tucked a strand of silky dark hair behind her ear. "Well, I did say yes. I did care about each one of them. I did think I could make it work but I was wrong. I did try to push back the feeling in my heart that they weren't you. But nobody was you and you'd hurt me deeply. You left me without a backward glance--"

"I--" His belly churned.

She held up a hand. "Let me finish. I cared about each one and I wanted it to be enough. It was safer, right? Safer to keep it on that level knowing that I wouldn't be abandoned again. But each time, in different ways, I realized before it had gone too far with the wedding planning, that I wasn't being fair to them. That I didn't love them in the way they deserved."

"So they were all good guys?"

She frowned and dropped her gaze to her hands. "Two out of three. One turned out to not handle the break-up well."

He tensed at the tone of her voice. "What happened?"

She shrugged but didn't meet his gaze. "It doesn't matter. Thomas turned out to be a jerk who couldn't accept that I'd left him. It's a non-issue now and I'd rather not discuss it."

Cam didn't like it but what could he say? He'd left and had no right to question her on anything. Even though if he ever found out this Thomas guy had hurt her, he'd personally kick his ass.

"Thanks for telling me. What about now?"

She looked up, her eyes wide. "Now?"

"Are you open to getting involved now?" He held his breath.

She set down her wine and her dark eyebrows rose. "Well,

I'm focused on this new job and really need to give it all my attention. Sound familiar?"

His lips quirked. "Yeah, I get it." He shifted in the chair, his mind whirring.

"I've spilled my guts to you, but was it only fear that made you act so cold?" She picked up her glass and took a healthy sip.

"Because I'm an idiot. Everything came rushing back seeing you with my family again. It hit me that I screwed up, that I'd hurt you, that I'd maybe ruined any chance I had at a life with my ride or die."

She sucked in a sharp inhale. "Your ride or die?"

It was now or never. "That's the term you used, right? I'm thirty-five but you're the only one I'd ever consider to be that person for me."

"Cam." Her melted-chocolate eyes gleamed in the light.

"You've been right about everything. I have been afraid. I have pushed people away. I know I don't deserve another chance, but I have to ask." He rose from the chair and crossed to the couch, without breaking her gaze.

He hesitated, allowing his eyes to reveal his emotions, to offer a hint of vulnerability. "Lucy, will you give me another chance? Could we try and see where this goes?"

She reached up, caught his hand and stood. "Just live in the present right now, and see what happens?"

He searched her face, looking for clues. "Whatever you want. Can I take you out on a date tomorrow night? A fresh start?"

She nodded. "I'd love to go out with you. Let's try dating for now. Now kiss me."

He cupped her beautiful face in his hands, leaned down and slanted his mouth against hers. Her petal soft lips parted, her breath sweet and warm and inviting. She pressed closer to him and wound her arms around his neck. He groaned, threaded his fingers through her silky hair and tugged her closer. Lost in her delicate lemony scent. Lost in her.

She murmured against his mouth. "Let's go to my room."

Every muscle in his body leapt to attention. No way could he refuse her request, even if it meant revealing his insecurities. Even if it meant unveiling his scars to her.

Being with Lucy was worth the risk.

CHAPTER 14

ucy's heart hammered against her ribs and warmth suffused her body. Cam's grip on her hand was firm and sure. Excitement and nerves warred for control within her, but she shook them away. She'd dreamt of this moment––the moment she'd be in his powerful arms again.

They crossed to her Queen-sized bed and together they sank into the fluffy duvet and firm mattress. Cam rolled onto his back and his strong hands clasped her hips, lifting her on top of him in one smooth move. Even fully dressed, the heat from his body flamed through her, pooling low in her belly. She tightened her thighs around him, her muscles clenching. Their gazes remained locked as she lowered her head and brushed her lips against his.

He growled low in his throat and his hands stroked up her waist to span her ribcage. Her nipples leapt to attention and she sighed into the kiss, slow and tender, like they had all the time in the world. He tugged her closer, his grip tight. The kiss transformed from gentle and whisper-soft to hot passionate possession. She moaned and allowed him to take control, reveling in his strength.

She rocked her hips against the steel ridge of his erection, a flash of feminine power sparking through her veins. His chest rumbled and he grasped the hem of her top and whipped it off. His crystal blue eyes darkened with desire as they raked over her. He tugged her closer and flicked his tongue across her taut nipples, sending sparks of sensation through her system.

Her back bowed and her mind blanked. His talented mouth nibbled and kissed and drove her wild. His firm grip held her in place while he devoured her. Her nails dug into his strong shoulders. She was lost. Lost in his powerful embrace. Lost in the heat of his passionate kisses. Lost in the present with the man she loved.

She wanted more. Needed more. "I need to feel you against me. Take off your shirt."

He tore off his long-sleeved Henley, revealing his sculpted from marble body. She stroked her fingers along his chiseled pecs, down the defined ridges of his abs, and those Vs of muscle disappearing into the waistband of his jeans. She tightened the grip of her thighs and leaned back far enough to flip the top button of his jeans open.

"Lucy." He reached for her, drawing her down so her breasts crushed against him. She sighed and melted into his hot, smooth skin. She turned her head and kissed the spot where his neck and shoulder met, inhaling his clean masculine scent. He jolted and slid his hands down to her bottom and pressed her even closer to his hard length.

"I want you inside me, Cam. I don't want to wait." An urgency filled her. An urgency to anchor them in the present together.

"Not yet." He rolled them to the side, propped up on one elbow, his eyes hooded. "I've got to taste you first."

Her breath caught in her throat and she shifted, eager and ready.

He lowered his head and trailed open-mouthed kisses along her collarbone, liquid fire against her skin. Her head dropped to the side, her back arched into his touch. Continuing his assault, he caught one breast in his mouth, teasing her sensitive nipple, and traced his long fingers down her belly until he cupped her through her jeans.

Her hips jerked upwards into his hand. "Cam." His name escaped on a breathless moan.

He unfastened her jeans, sliding them down. She lifted her hips and reached down to help shove them off. He traced his fingers along the edge of her lacy thong and tugged it free.

"Let me look at you. You are so beautiful, Lucy. More beautiful than my dreams of you." His gaze was reverent.

"So are you." She lifted her arms, goosebumps erupting on her now cool skin.

He lowered his head and rained kisses down her torso, from the tender underside of her breast, along her belly, and then exhaled on the hollow of her hipbone.

She shifted, restless, hungry, eager. "You're teasing me."

He looked up, his mouth poised mere inches from her aching center, his gaze wicked now. "Is this what you want?"

"Please." The word escaped on a gasp of pleasure.

He flashed a wicked grin and licked her once, twice, before giving all his attention to pleasuring her. His hands held her hips in place, and she lost herself in the waves of sensation flowing through her. Her fingers dug into his hair, pressing him deeper, and he groaned his approval. Every muscle in her body trembled and pressure built until stars burst behind her eyes and she stiffened and cried his name.

Once she'd stilled, Cam slid up her body and captured her mouth. She raked her fingernails down his back and savored the feeling of him against her. "Let me return the favor."

"I won't make it. I need to be inside you now." He growled.

Her muscles clenched. "Condoms in my nightstand drawer. Let me get them." She rolled to the side and bumped into his legs.

He winced and cursed under his breath.

"Are you okay?" She held her breath--not again.

"Yeah. Just give me a second. My thigh." He hissed through gritted teeth.

"Oh my god, I'm so sorry. What can I do?" She scrambled off the bed. Seeing him in pain hurt her heart--a reminder of how much his life had changed since they were together last.

He sat up and dropped his head in his hands. "I'm okay now but maybe I should go."

She scooted next to him and rubbed her hand along his leanly muscled back. "No, you shouldn't. Does it still hurt?"

He turned his head and looked up at her. "It's feeling pretty sore."

For Cam to admit something was causing him pain meant that it must be excruciating. He'd hate it if she made a big deal out of it and tried to baby him, so she made a split-second decision.

She leaned in and whispered in his ear, "I think you being buried deep inside me will make everything better." She placed one hand against his broad shoulder and gently pushed.

He inhaled sharply, his eyes widened, but he didn't resist. His eyes were hooded, and he reached to unzip his pants and shove them down his legs. She tugged at the hems and helped him slide out of the restrictive denim and boxer briefs.

The material caught on his prosthetic, and she gently guided it off and pushed his clothes to the floor. "Do you want to keep your limb on or off?"

"On. Come back up here." Cam's raspy voice held a hint of vulnerability.

"One second." She popped up and grabbed a condom from her nightstand drawer and crawled back onto the bed and straddled him.

His jaw was tight, his breath coming in staccato bursts. She leaned back and helped him sheath his impressive erection. They'd hit a snag, but he'd see she'd been telling the truth——he was sexier than ever.

She lowered herself, inch by beautiful inch, until they were completely connected. He intertwined his fingers with hers and grazed his mouth along their joined hands. His intense gaze seared through her.

Fire coursed through her veins, her eyelids floated shut, and she threw her head back and rode him. Their skin grew slick, and tingles of pleasure intensified within her.

She matched him stroke for stroke, reveling in how perfectly he filled her.

"Come for me, Lucy." He reached his hand between them, stroking the spot where they were joined. "Now."

She tumbled over the edge, and he followed her, her name on his lips.

When she remembered to breathe again, she pressed her mouth against his sweat-dampened skin. He wrapped one sinewy arm around her and hugged her tight. For a moment, their mingled breath was the only sound in the room.

She lifted her head and gazed into his heavy-lidded blue eyes. "That was amazing."

His eyes crinkled at the corners and his lips curved upwards. "Yeah, it was. You are amazing."

Happiness bloomed in her chest——the reality of making love with him again surpassed the fantasies she'd harbored over the last decade. "I've missed you."

His expression grew more serious. "Lucy, it's only ever been you. But let me get up and take care of things."

She eased off him. He rose and headed toward the bathroom. She admired the way his broad shoulders tapered into narrow hips, to his high round perfect butt.

Even though they hadn't been together for years, there had been a recognition, a sense of coming home the moment they'd touched. Making love to Cameron felt right. Natural. If anything, their chemistry had intensified.

She'd always believed they were soul mates and when he'd left her, she figured he didn't feel the same way. But now, with his actions and his words, he was demonstrating that she'd been right all along. Reuniting in Monterey was destiny at work. Just like that book from the 90s, *The Celestine Prophecy*, that hinged on the premise there were no coincidences.

Energized, she bounded off the bed. Suddenly, she wanted to pop a bottle of champagne and celebrate.

Cam appeared in the doorway, gloriously naked. "Is that beautiful smile just for me?" He flashed a boyish grin, looking years younger than he had earlier this week.

She sauntered toward him. "Why yes, it is. I want champagne, you in?"

"Champagne?"

She stepped onto her tiptoes and wound her arms around his strong neck. She tilted her head back and beamed. "Champagne is a vital ingredient to any proper celebration and being with you again makes me happy."

He leaned down and threaded his fingers through her hair. He slanted his mouth against hers, his kiss deep and possessive. "Me too," he whispered against her lips.

She took a step back. "I'm grabbing my robe from the bathroom and popping the cork. Feel free to stay in your birthday suit." She raked her gaze down his supremely fine body and waggled her eyebrows.

His lips twitched. "I'll grab my jeans and meet you on the couch."

Her heart light, she floated to the kitchen to open the bubbly and toast to their reconciliation. She poured the fizzy liquid into two flutes and carried them to the couch. She set both glasses down on the coffee table and sank into the fluffy cushions.

Her phone buzzed but she ignored it. When it started up again, she grabbed it and checked the text messages pouring in. Victoria Harrington had shared her Instagram post declaring she was getting married at Cypress Coast Ranch along with one indicating they'd emailed the signed contract to her.

"Yes." She pumped her fist.

Her breath caught in her throat when Cam approached looking just as sexy from the front as he had from the back, his lean, muscular chest bare, the treasure trail of dark blond hair disappearing into the unfastened top button of his jeans.

He sank onto the couch next to her, handed her a glass, and lifted his. "Now I like that enthusiasm. To the most incredible woman I've ever met."

"I'll drink to that. But more good news--the Harringtons finally signed the contract. We won." She grinned and took a sip. "My turn. To the reality of you being better than the dream version."

He quirked a brow. "I knew it. But tell me about the dream version?"

She scooted closer to him. "My memories. It's just so surreal to be with you this way again--I dreamt about you a lot. Fantasized about seeing you again. And here we are."

"I dreamt of you too." He laced his fingers with hers and squeezed.

Her pulse accelerated but she didn't respond, just took another sip. Did he really mean it when he said he'd never been in love with another woman? His admission was enough for now. If he wanted to elaborate or go deeper, she'd let him set the pace.

"Want another glass?" She started to rise.

He shook his head and set his flute on the table. "No more for me. I need to drive home."

"You aren't going to stay over?"

"Not tonight. I've got to get Frank home and I've got an early morning." He stood, pulled her to her feet and into his arms. "I had an amazing time tonight."

She met his gaze. "Me too." Although she'd been looking forward to falling asleep with him, she would take this one step at a time. If they were destined to be together, it would happen. For now, she'd savor his sincere words and their beautiful lovemaking and ignore the pang in her heart at his departure.

CHAPTER 15

"Sue, I've got the food and I need you to come over pronto, please? Emergency meeting," Lucy struggled not to bellow into the phone. Now was not the time for her best friend to dawdle. She'd burst if she didn't share the recent developments with Cam.

"I'll be there in fifteen, okay? Just pour a big vat of wine and take some deep breaths."

"Easy for you to say." She glared at the phone, but Sue had already hung up.

Lucy marched to her wine refrigerator and perused the contents. On one hand, tonight was a celebration but on the other, she was totally freaking out.

Maybe she could call Campbell and ask her what sommeliers recommended in circumstances where exes slept together again after more than a decade? She snorted--like Campbell would reply, "Why yes, I have the perfect vintage for that."

Lucy tapped a finger on her chin and concentrated-- definitely something expensive, fancy, and delicious. She'd been preaching about living life in the present moment so why not break out the Tuscan Brunello she'd been saving for a special occasion?

If her first love asking her for a second chance didn't qualify, what would? With a decisive nod, she pulled the wine off the rack.

She uncorked the bottle and poured it in a crystal decanter to breathe until Sue arrived. Decanting would ensure the wine opened properly so they could savor every drop. While she waited, she pulled out her sunflower-patterned dishes and split their favorite grilled salmon salad, sliced the half baguette, and grabbed two large glasses of water.

The front door burst open, and Sue rolled inside on an icy blast of Monterey wind. "It's freezing out there. Tell me you picked up something hearty like beef stew or meatloaf for dinner."

Lucy laughed. "Sorry, I got salmon salad. But I do have a fresh baguette, if that will help. And I opened the Brunello we picked up in Italy on our amazing trip five years ago."

Sue's bluebell eyes widened. "This is serious if you opened that bottle. Excuse the outfit, I was in reno hell all day and needed comfort." She unwound her scarf to reveal an ancient Yale sweatshirt and red plaid flannel pajama bottoms.

Lucy gestured down at her own p.js. "You may notice, I too am wearing my fanciest clothes. Only the best for you. But I can't believe you're still wearing Biff's sweatshirt. I thought you burned it."

Sue crossed the room and squeezed her in a quick hug. "Ha ha. Biff. Brock's sweatshirt has reached a level of softness that nothing can rival. I don't even think about that cheating troll when I wear it."

Sue's boyfriend right after college had been an uptight ass who'd managed to insert "Yale" into almost any conversation, no matter how unrelated. When he'd been fired from his job for screwing his assistant in the company restroom, Sue had dumped him. And luckily, he disappeared, never to be heard from again.

Lucy waved a hand. "Good riddance Biff-Brock. More important matters to discuss tonight. I've got to tell you about Cam."

"What about Cam?" Sue stepped back and peered at her. "Hold on a minute. You had sex with him, didn't you?"

Lucy's cheeks grew warm. "Why else do you think I called an emergency meeting? And I told him about Greg, Thomas, and Sean."

Sue's jaw fell open. "Okay, pour the wine. This I've got to hear. Are you okay?"

Lucy nodded. "Let me start at the beginning. It started out rough last weekend, got rougher, and then it all turned around last night."

She poured generous--some might say gluttonous--goblets of wine for them both. They moved to the couch. Dinner could wait until after her first download of information.

"So you know about the walk when I kissed him. Told you the chemistry is as explosive as it was before. Then we had a meeting with the bridezilla, who picked me up in a limo and left me stranded."

Sue raised her glass. "But you got the deal, right? Congratulations girl!"

"Yes, they sent the contract over and she posted it on Instagram so it must be real. So happy." They clinked glasses and Lucy took a sip. "Cam offered to drive me home and we went to his house to feed Frank and ended up getting pizza. Without taking an hour, let's just say we got into it about the past, about his feelings being an amputee, and I told him I'd been engaged three times. We kissed again--made out for a while actually––and then he retreated again, said kissing me was a mistake. I lost it on him and left. Then I went to Sunday dinner with the Taylors."

"Whew. Why was the kiss a mistake? He's single, right?" Sue's eyes narrowed.

Lucy wrinkled her nose. "Because of our past? Because he hasn't been in a serious relationship since ours. Because we're working together now and there's a lot at stake for the hotel. Pick one."

Sue shook her head. "Well, it isn't exactly straightforward with you two."

"Right? And I may or may not have said something about I broke up with the guys because they weren't him." Lucy cleared her throat.

"Oh." Sue drew out the word into about four syllables.

Lucy nodded. "Well, he made me so angry because he admitted he'd made the decision to break up with me partially to protect me––no discussion, just oh, let me protect poor delicate little Lucy. I swear, I'm sunshine and kittens and he can trigger my temper like no one else."

Sue snorted. "Sunshine and kittens with a steel spine. Yeah, well that's probably part of your chemistry. He makes you feel different than anyone else has or can."

"Yes! So, Sunday I'm a nervous wreck going to the Taylors. Austin, Lucas, Jack, and Campbell are all in town. And I haven't seen Cam's dad in so long. It was wonderful and awful at the same time. They really were like my second family. Everyone was lovely and Cam just sat there and ignored me, like a total ass."

Sue gave her an owlish stare. "Ass! You're cussing so he must have been a total asshat. Go on."

Lucy sniffed. She could curse once in a while. It wasn't like she was some Puritan or something.

"After a few awkward encounters at work, last night he

showed up at my doorstep with that irresistible dog and asked if he could come in and apologize."

"Hmm…" Sue picked up her wineglass and drank.

"He was genuine and opened up more than I'm used to with him. And then one thing led to another and boom. Best sex I've had in thirteen years." And wasn't that an outrageous understatement? More like mind-blowing and panty-melting.

Sue's eyebrows flew up to her hairline. "Best sex since Cam Version 1.0?"

Lucy giggled. "Yeah, Cam Version 2.0 blew my mind. I can't even describe the feeling, but it was like coming home and also like taking a wild new ride. Familiar yet new and exhilarating at the same time."

"Did he spend the night? Are you guys back together?"

Lucy's heart skipped a beat. "He went home in the middle of the night, but we've got a date tomorrow night." She'd been disappointed but she suspected he was uncomfortable removing his artificial limb in front of her.

Sue set down her glass, leaned in, and grabbed her hand. She searched her eyes. "Tell me how you're feeling. Deep down. Tell me."

Lucy inhaled deeply, exhaled slowly. "I'm excited and terrified and hopeful this is it. Maybe I need to go for it and see if Cam truly is my soul mate. If we're meant to be. Or maybe this is a complete disaster and I'm going to screw up my dream job and lose Cam all over again."

Sue squeezed her fingers. "I'm excited and scared for you, too. Promise me you'll take your time?"

Lucy pressed one hand to her heart. "We talked a lot about living in the present moment. I think we're going to date. Like instead of a high school couple who grew up 'going together,' we're going to start over as the people we've grown into."

"Sounds very mature." Sue nodded.

"Oh Sue, nothing is like being with him. The same goose-bumps, the same sense of recognition. I still love him but I'm not going to tell him yet. I want us to end up together, but I've got to take it one day at a time. He's got some stuff he's still contending with from being overseas and I'm not sure he's healed yet."

"Again, very mature. And you do have time. And if he hurts you again, I'm going to personally kick his ass." Sue shook a fist in the air.

Lucy threw her head back and laughed, just like her best friend intended. "You've never punched anyone in your life but thank you. I'll allow it. And I'm starved."

"Well, I'm happy for you but there's a first time for every-thing and if he deserves it, I will make him pay. And I am also starving. Let's eat and watch *Bridesmaids*, deal?"

Lucy groaned. "We've seen that movie at least twenty times. But fine."

The Harringtons could star in their own version of the romantic comedy. But she wouldn't think about them tonight. She'd enjoy dinner with her bestie. Sharing every-thing with Sue had filled her with a sense of calm, despite her friend's concern.

Nobody would quash her excitement about being back together with Cam. Not even her own niggling doubts.

CHAPTER 16

*B*etween meeting with contractors, interviewing potential staff, and slogging through his seemingly endless Cypress Coast Ranch to-do list, the last few weeks of January zipped by in a blur. But carving out time to surprise Lucy with a Valentine's Day afternoon picnic on the beach was worth the early hours Cam had been logging.

He parked in front of her cottage and nerves skittered down his spine. He'd been essentially fearless as a soldier, and now he was worried Lucy might not welcome an interruption during her busy day. He exhaled, grabbed the pink tulips, and exited his Jeep. Although a chill hung in the blue-gray sky, the afternoon sun warmed his back, and the customary breeze wasn't whipping through the trees.

He ignored his accelerated pulse, tucked the bouquet behind his back, and knocked on her front door.

She opened the door and her enormous chocolate brown eyes rounded. "Cam? You're four hours early."

He swept the flowers out with a flourish and smiled. "Happy Valentine's Day, beautiful."

Her eyes sparkled and her full lips parted. "You remembered tulips were my favorite but I thought I wouldn't see you until tonight?"

"Surprise. The boss is giving you the day off." He handed her the bouquet. "You just need to put on some warm clothes."

A rosy flush rose in her cheeks, and she pressed one hand to her chest. "I don't know what to say."

He stepped forward, cupped her delicate jaw in his hands, and slanted his mouth across hers and murmured, "Say, please come inside and I'll change and be ready in five minutes."

Lucy smiled into the kiss. "Five minutes is pushing it, but I'll see what I can do."

She backed into the cottage and he followed, pushing the door shut behind him. Her shiny dark hair was held away from her gorgeous face with a big plastic clip, she wore baggy sweats, a SFSU sweatshirt, and yellow polka-dot socks. She looked freakin' adorable.

"Tell me where a vase is and I'll put the flowers in water while you change. Or you can wear what you've got on." Although, unwrapping her layers and staying in bed for the next four hours was tempting.

She snorted. "Nice try. These are strictly my work-from-home clothes, at least where no video meetings are involved. I'll throw on some jeans and a sweater."

"Five minutes. We've got a schedule."

She saluted him with a sassy grin, then disappeared into her bedroom. "Yes sir."

He organized the flowers, then sat on the couch and scrolled through email on his phone to ensure no fires needed extinguishing at the hotel. Nothing was marked urgent--so far, so good.

Lucy sauntered into the room, looking delicious. "Let me grab my purse and I'll be ready."

He rose, anticipation mounting for their afternoon plans. Even though pouncing on her and ravishing her on the couch was tempting, he'd promised himself he'd give Lucy flowers and romance. With a backward glance at the sofa, he clasped her hand and they headed to his car.

Cam glanced over at Lucy and an unfamiliar sense of contentment filled him. She looked gorgeous in a snug white turtleneck with a red heart on her chest, dark jeans, and knee-high sheepskin boots. No question––he was a lucky bastard she was giving him another chance and he'd wanted to do something romantic for her. Something unexpected.

She reached across the Jeep's console and caught his hand and interlaced her slender fingers with his. "I'm excited to spend the afternoon with you. I thought we'd agreed on a quiet night at my place with my special lasagna. And lucky for you I made said lasagna last night, so it only needs heating up. Will you tell me where we're going?"

"That would ruin the surprise, right?" He grinned when she pouted and jerked his thumb toward the wicker picnic basket in the back seat. It was crammed full of charcuterie, cheeses, and Lucy's favorite strawberry tarts. "There's a hint."

She angled toward him and clapped her hands together. "You put together a picnic? Are we going to the wharf? The gardens at the hotel? The beach?" Enthusiasm laced her voice.

He placed one hand on her slender denim-clad thigh and squeezed. "Yes, and it's a surprise."

He navigated down the side streets until he reached Hwy. 1 and headed south to Carmel by-the-Sea, which had the most beautiful beach set inside rugged cliffs. With each mile along the winding coastal road, his shoulders relaxed, and the responsibilities of work receded in the rear view.

Lucy's phone beeped and she fished it out of her purse.

"Sorry, just need to make sure there aren't any pressing issues." Her brow furrowed, and tapped out a reply.

"Everything okay?" He wanted today to be perfect.

She frowned, blew out a breath, then glanced over at him. "Everything's fine. Just Victoria Harrington wondering if she could require all the guests to wear the exact same shade of iris purple to match her wedding flowers. And list that on the wedding invitations."

"What?" He might not know much about weddings, but he'd been to a few, and this ask sounded ridiculous.

Lucy rolled her eyes. "I told her she could, but it would be impossible to monitor. And she wants the guys in purple suits, like Violet from Willy Wonka? So, are we going to Carmel? Remember when you took me there the weekend before I started college?"

"That was a fun one and yes. And I said it before but your job is interesting."

She nodded and gazed out the passenger window just as a flash of pale sand beach and white-capped surf appeared between the Monterey cypress trees. "It comes with the territory. I just have to keep my sense of humor. But enough about bridezilla. It's absolutely breathtaking down here. Thanks for getting us out of town for a bit."

He cruised down the main street of Carmel and scored a parking space just steps from the sand. "I figured we could walk along the beach path and have a picnic watching for dolphins."

They exited his Jeep and traversed to the paved path that ran along the long, wide coastline. The chilly wind was punctuated by crashing waves and squawking seagulls. He led them to a bench beneath one of the gnarled trees dotted along the stretch of coastline, one of his favorite secluded spots with an unobstructed view of the jagged cliffs and turbulent cerulean sea.

"This is amazing--I love that it's away from the busier parts of the beach. It's like our own private cove." She held up one hand and surveyed the scenery. A strand of dark hair blew across her ivory cheek.

He brushed her hair aside and tucked it behind her ear, then pulled her into his arms. "Exactly. Close enough, anyway."

He cupped her face in his hands and claimed her mouth. Her lips parted on a sigh, he deepened the kiss, and her tongue swept around his, tasting, discovering, savoring. She smelled like lemon and sunshine, and her passionate response made him go rock hard.

After a few satisfying minutes, he lifted his head. Plans--picnic, romance, words--he needed to focus. Their first Valentine's Day together again after so long needed to be special. He'd wasted too many opportunities to romance Lucy--no more. He caught her hand and drew her down beside him on the bench.

She flipped open the picnic basket and rubbed her hands together. "I'm starving. This looks amazing. All my favorites and you even sliced up the Manchego and Gouda. Who knew you were so domestic?"

His lips twitched. "Yeah, that's me. Mr. Domestic. Just practical. But before we dig in, I need to tell you something."

"It better be important if it takes precedence over cheese," she said with a sly grin.

"You know I'm not always great with words but here goes." His heart thundered in his chest, and he inhaled a deep breath. "I've missed you so much. Every day we spend together, I realize how wild I am about you. How bad I messed up."

Lucy gasped and her chocolate brown eyes widened. "Cam, I've missed you too."

Encouraged, he forged on. "I know I hurt you but I'm a

different man now. I'm still battling PTSD and learning to live a very different life. But you were right all along, and we have something special. Something that doesn't come along often. Will you be able to put the past behind and give me the chance to make you happy?"

Her cheeks flushed and she caught her lower lip in her white teeth. "I told you that I wanted to be with you again. We're dating. I wouldn't be here with you otherwise."

Heat radiated down his spine. "I want to make sure you know that I love you. That I've never stopped loving you. And despite knowing I don't deserve you, I want to prove to you that you can trust me to be here for you."

Her breath hitched. "Say it again." She moved the picnic basket onto the ground and scooted closer to him.

"Which part? The part about you being right?"

Her eyes narrowed, and she swatted him. "Tell me you love me again."

"I love you, Lucy Goodwin." Joy spread through his chest. "I love you."

She laughed and threw her arms around his neck. "I love you, Cameron Taylor. And I love being right. Kiss me, please."

He lowered his mouth and she met him halfway, parting her eager lips beneath his, her breath sweet and hot. Her stomach grumbled and she pulled back. "And I am hungry. I don't want you to think I don't appreciate all your hard work."

He chuckled, his whole being filled with a sense of lightness. "Yeah, that would be rude. I stayed up late slicing cheese for you."

She laid her hand on his forearm, her touch singeing him through his down jacket. "Seriously, thanks for this surprise. I love it. And what a treat to spend the afternoon and tonight with you. You're sure we can play hooky from the hotel this long?"

He shrugged. "Everyone's got their assignments and if one afternoon breaks it all, we're in trouble, right?"

"Look at you, all casual. I like seeing you more relaxed. It suits you." She beamed at him before she placed some prosciutto di parma and Manchego on a baguette slice and took a bite. "Mmm…perfect."

Cam basked in the perfect moment--he'd declared his love, he'd chosen to take time to be with Lucy instead of burying all his energy into work--life was good.

AFTER AN INCREDIBLE AFTERNOON and an even more incredible lasagna dinner, Cam and Lucy were sprawled on her couch. Mellow piano music played in the background and his 5 a.m. wake-up was catching up him. His eyelids floated shut and he dropped his head back on the soft cushions.

"We're both exhausted and I've got the perfect solution-- a bubble bath in my claw-footed bathtub." Lucy leaned against him and traced her fingers in lazy circles down his chest. Every muscle in his body stiffened.

"A bath? Is that tub big enough for both of us?" A prickle of unease slid down his spine--taking a bath meant removing his prosthetic. Although he'd taken it off the other night and she'd seen it, he still felt awkward.

"Mmm-hmm…steaming hot water and lots of bubbles. I know you'll love it."

"I love you." He trailed kisses down to her collarbone and brushed his thumb against her pebbled nipple.

She turned her head and gazed at him with her soft

chocolate eyes. "I love you and I'd love to be all slick and wet in the tub with you. I promise you'll enjoy it."

"I can make you slick, and wet right here." He slid one hand down and cupped her.

Her head dropped back, she arched against him, and murmured. "Please?"

He sighed. "How can I ever tell you no? Go run the bath and I'll be right in." He'd have to remove his limb in the bathroom. Time to get over himself and just do it, the leg wasn't growing back.

She popped up from the couch. "Meet me in there in five minutes." Her pink lips curved up into a teasing grin.

He waited a few minutes and followed her in. She'd set the scene with dozens of candles and steamy bubbles floating at the top of the bathtub. She turned toward him, stretched up onto her tiptoes, and brushed a feather-light kiss across his lips. "You get in and I'll be right back. I'm pouring us a glass of wine."

His shoulders relaxed––her sensitivity and consideration offering him privacy rendered her even more beautiful. He shucked his clothes and his artificial limb, leaving them in a tidy pile on the vanity. He carefully slid into the water, hissed at the heat but after a moment adjusted and settled at one end of the tub. He closed his eyes and rested his head back against the cool rim.

"See, not so bad, is it?"

He opened his eyes and there she stood, looking delicious wearing nothing, and holding two glasses of red wine. His cock leapt to attention. "You were right, as usual. Now get in here with me."

"Hold the wine, please." She leaned forward, her alabaster skin gleaming in the candlelight.

Their fingers brushed, shooting a jolt of electricity through him. He gripped the glasses and heat coursed through his veins. She took her time, dipping one foot into the water, before slowly lowering her tempting body into the tub. She settled across with him and slid her toned legs between his thighs.

"Happy to see me?" Her eyes hooded and she brushed one foot back and forth along his inner thigh.

He caught her slender ankle and tugged. "You could say that. Why don't you come closer?" He placed both glasses on the small ledge next to the tub. He couldn't wait another minute for her.

Her pupils flared and she shifted forward, wrapped her fingers around the edge of the tub, and carefully straddled him. She sank down until her core pressed into his aching hard erection. "Is this close enough?"

His back bowed and he wrapped his hands around her hips. "No. I need you now, Lucy."

"Yes. Now." She braced her hands on his shoulders and rocked her weight forward.

He guided her down slowly and her muscles clenched around him. She fit like she was made just for him. "Lucy." He hissed between gritted teeth.

She slid her hands up, caught his face, and kissed him, her soft lips and sweet breath mesmerizing him. Their tongues tangled and stroked in a lazy dance while he held her still. She began to ride, matching the slow pace of their kiss, rising up and down at a dreamlike pace. He cupped her tight little ass and picked up their pace.

The bubbles splashed and sloshed around them, their kisses grew deeper, wilder, hotter. She dug her fingers into his hair, the slight pain spurring him on.

He tilted her hips to ensure he was giving her the angle he knew drove her wild. Her body began to vibrate, tremors pulsating around him until he felt his own release start to climb. Sensation shot up from the base of his spine just as she exploded and cried his name against his mouth.

Unable to hold back, he followed her over the edge with a guttural moan. He dropped his head onto her shoulder, tracing her damp, salty skin with his tongue. His heart hammered against his ribs and his breath came in sharp, ragged bursts.

Lucy Goodwin blew his mind. How had he ever believed he could live without her?

She ran her fingers through his sweat-dampened hair and brushed feather-light kisses along the sensitive skin below his ear. He shivered, wrapped his arms tighter around her so he couldn't distinguish where she began and he ended. He captured her mouth, her sweet breath mingling with his, their tongues playing, dancing, savoring.

She pulled back, her eyelids heavy, her lips curved upward in a satisfied smile. "So, I take it you approve of the bubble bath?"

He nodded. "Absolutely."

"See, I told you I was right, again. Now I'm hungry for dessert...should we have some gelato?"

He laughed. "I'm still inside you, woman, and you're thinking about gelato?"

She winked. "What can I say? I'm indulging myself tonight. How about gelato in bed?"

"Whatever you want." He pressed his lips to hers in a playful kiss. "You have to let me out of here first, I'm trapped."

She smiled against his mouth before levering out of the tub. "Let's do it. We've got all night. Meet me in the bedroom."

"Lucy, I'm not sure I should stay over." He hadn't slept at her house yet, too stressed over all the possibilities of what could go wrong.

She paused and pulled on a short, flowered robe and belted it around her tiny waist. "Cam, please stay. You haven't spent the night with me and I want to wake up in your arms."

He leaned his head against the hard rim of the tub and sighed. "I'm worried I won't be able to sleep or if I do sleep, I could hurt you during one of my nightmares." He'd never forgive himself.

Lucy approached the tub and knelt so her beautiful face was level with his. "Did you ever consider that sleeping here with me might help your nightmares stop?"

Cam's breath lodged in his throat--this second chance with Lucy was more than he imagined. More than he deserved. He reached out one hand and stroked his fingertips along her silky cheek. "You're sure?"

She turned her head and kissed his palm. "I'm sure. I'll see you in the bedroom."

He watched her gracefully rise and stroll out of the bathroom on her shapely stems. Maybe with Lucy's belief in him, he could face his PTSD head on and who knows, maybe one day rid himself of it forever. An unfamiliar sense of peace filled him.

Tonight, he'd stay with her and hoped he'd be able to sleep without nightmares. Life with Lucy Goodwin was worth facing his demons.

CHAPTER 17

"Thanks so much for agreeing to see me. You look incredible, Lucy." Greg reached for her hand across the small round wooden table. He smiled broadly as his blue eyes searched her face.

Lucy snatched her hand back and intertwined her fingers together in her lap. Agreeing to meet Ex-Fiancé #3 for coffee because he was in town on business was one thing. Touching him was another. "Thanks. So, how's it going? When you texted me, you said you were in Monterey on business and had something important to discuss?"

She studied his square-jawed face and wondered how she'd ever seen a resemblance to Cam. Sure, their blond coloring and lean muscular frames were similar but where her pulse hammered in her throat when she was close to Cam, nothing happened with Greg.

After the horrible break-up with Thomas, Ex-Fiancé #2, who had been an emotionally abusive gaslighter, she'd been thrilled to date Greg, who was one of the nicest guys she'd ever met. He was sweet, considerate, stable…and honestly, a little boring.

At the time, she'd welcomed the way they had a regular schedule of dinner twice a week and sleepovers on the week-end. For the first six months, she'd basked in his gentle attention and their reliable routine. When he'd helped her change her number and ensured that Thomas's harassment stopped, she'd been grateful.

They wanted the same things in life––fulfilling careers, marriage, children, and no drama. On paper, they were compatible––a perfect match. She had loved him, in a mellow way. If being with him sometimes felt more like being with a close friend, that was okay, right?

After the way Cam had abandoned her and the way Thomas had tried to control her, being with Greg had been like a soothing balm. No more intense highs and low, just sweet and steady. She'd stepped off the rollercoaster forever.

She'd convinced herself it would be enough, even though one part of her heart remained untouched when she was with him. She'd convinced herself they could build a lovely life together. Excitement could come from travel or work or her girlfriends.

Greg shrugged and gave a sheepish smile. "Well, not really. But I needed to drive through on the way down to Cambria and I've missed you so much these past months."

She gazed down at her café au lait and sighed. "Greg, we broke up over a year ago. You said you needed to talk to me and it was important."

"I know, but how can I not miss you? We were good together. I know you weren't ready then but maybe the timing is right now. I think we should give us another try." He leaned in toward the table, hope shimmering in his eyes.

She exhaled an unsteady breath. She didn't want to hurt him more than she already had. "Greg, I––"

"Lucy, I've dated other women but none of them are you. You're it for me. Ending our engagement was a mistake. If you give me a second chance, we could build a great life together." His voice grew urgent.

"Oh, Greg." Her heart contracted. "You're such a great guy and I enjoyed our time together so much, but this is my fault. I shouldn't have agreed to marry you."

He jerked his head back sat back. "Wow. Don't sugarcoat it."

"I'm sorry. That came out wrong. Please know it isn't anything you did or didn't do. My heart has never been whole and while I did love you, one part still belongs to my ex."

"Belongs?" His mouth snapped shut.

May as well be brutally honest. "Yes, belongs. I'm seeing him again."

His jaw dropped and his voice rose. "Wasn't your ex an abusive asshole? The guy I helped you get away from?"

She grimaced and shook her head. "Oh no, not Thomas. My first ex, Cameron."

"The guy who dumped you to dedicate his life to the military? Over a decade ago?" His brow furrowed.

Lucy bit her lip and nodded. What had she been thinking, agreeing to meet him today? Maybe that he'd tell her he'd moved on too and she didn't need to feel guilty for hurting him? Big mistake.

He raked his fingers through his thick golden hair and his jaw tightened. "So, you were in love with him even though you got engaged to me? Did you even mean it when you told me you loved me?"

She squeezed her eyes shut and took a cleansing breath. "Yes, I meant it when I said I loved you. I cared about you, I liked you, I was attracted to you. I did mean it. But I broke it off because you deserve someone who will love you with their entire being and I realized that person wasn't me. Can you ever forgive me?"

He looked away and shook his head. "I don't know. You weren't honest with me. I never would have proposed if I didn't think you loved me the way I loved you."

"You had to sense it on some level, right?" Or was she simply attempting to assuage her guilt?

"I don't know. Maybe." He waved a hand in the air. "I thought we were happy."

She leaned forward and placed her hand on his forearm. "Greg, we were happy. I don't regret a minute we spent together but I do regret leading you on, even though that's not what I intended. I wanted you to be the one but when I realized I couldn't give you everything you deserve, that's when I broke it off. I'm so sorry."

And why couldn't she have fallen head over heels for him? But compatibility and chemistry didn't always go hand in hand. In the end, her heart wasn't hers to give to anyone other than Cameron Taylor.

A man cleared his throat next to them. Lucy whipped her head up and there stood Cam, looming over the table, his eyes narrowed, his jaw carved from stone.

"Cam, I thought you were at the hotel?" And that's the best she had?

His nostrils flared and his voice was deceptively quiet. "I was but I needed an extra hit of caffeine." He turned and glowered at Greg. "I'm Cam Taylor, who are you?"

Lucy's belly twisted and she shifted in her chair. Talk about terrible timing.

Greg's leaned back in his chair and lifted his chin. "Greg Sorenson. I take it you're the college ex?"

Cam crossed his arms over his broad chest and gave a curt nod.

"I'm one of the ex-fiancés. And I'm out of here. Have a nice life." Greg stood and marched out of the small café.

Cam stared down at her, his eyes frozen shards of ice.

"Sorry to interrupt your reunion. Were you going to tell me you were seeing that guy again?"

Lucy swallowed, her throat parched. "He texted the other day, said he'd be in town, and if you sit down, I can explain. Do you need to get your espresso first?"

"I don't want to talk about it here." He glanced around the noisy, crowded café. "I need to get back to the hotel."

Her heart pounded and perspiration beaded on the nape of her neck. "I've got to get back to work too. Can we discuss it there?"

He shook his head. "I don't have time."

"Okay, well, what time should I come over tonight? I was going to pick up dinner?" She managed to keep her voice level and the panic rising in her throat at bay.

He pivoted toward the coffee pick-up counter. "Not tonight. I'll be working late. Text me in a few days and we'll set something up."

Avoiding her gaze, he strode to the bar, grabbed his drink, and was out the door without a backward glance.

Lucy dropped her head in her hands. Darn it all, what were the odds of Cam showing up for coffee in the middle of the morning? Especially now that everything had been going so smoothly between them and he'd finally been comfortable enough to stay the night? And of course, while she was touching Greg. She should never have agreed to meet her ex.

"Oh, to be young again and have suitors battling for your affections." A frail woman's voice said.

Lucy lifted her gaze to see an adorable senior citizen with snowy white hair at the table next to her. "Heard that, did you? There's no battle. Just a misunderstanding."

The woman raised penciled-on eyebrows and sipped from her steaming mug. "I say go for the grumpy one who just stormed out. I'd let him boss me around any day."

Lucy laugh snorted. "I'll be sure to let him know I've got

competition." Humor always helped, especially when her heart was thundering against her ribs and her belly was twisted in knots.

She rose and wound her emerald green scarf around her neck, slipped into her long wool coat, and headed for the front door. Despite having a ton of work to do, now she'd have the attention-span of a gnat worrying over Cam. But she knew the way he processed things and chasing after him now wouldn't help matters. She'd give him some space and some time but her heart ached. They'd made so much progress in the last weeks.

She crossed to the exit, hurried to her car, and hugged her coat close when the icy breeze dug through her layers. Once she slid into her car, she flipped on the ignition, and blasted the heat. Her hands trembled on the steering wheel––time to go home and process whatever this morning had been.

Once she reached home, she headed inside to make some tea. Cam's reaction had both surprised her and if she were completely honest with herself, thrilled her a little bit. Not that there had ever been occasion for him to be jealous during their six years together, but she wasn't accustomed to him acting that way.

Now, he'd been driving forward with their relationship and made it clear he wanted to be with her. He'd let down his guard and taken a bath with her without his artificial limb and spent the night, which had gone smoothly. Each moment they spent together convinced her that fate had stepped in to award them a second chance at love. Today's debacle had to be just a blip on their path, right?

Because if he left her again, her heart would never recover.

～

CAM MASSAGED his pounding temples and squeezed his eyes shut--maybe if he stopped staring at the computer screen, the stabbing pain in his forehead would lessen. He cracked one eye open and peered at the spreadsheet. Nope, the numbers still looked like hieroglyphics. He surged to his feet and crossed to his office's enormous picture window.

The fog was deep charcoal and thick enough to appear impenetrable. It suited his current mood perfectly. Gray with an extra serving of black. He hadn't felt this dark since the day he realized he would resign his commission instead of remaining in the military. Sure, he could have stayed on active duty but after losing Private Hawkins and his own leg, he'd lost his motivation. The chapter of his life he'd envisioned lasting forever was forever closed.

Just like he'd believed his and Lucy's story had slammed shut all those years ago. After the way he'd left her, after his injury--he never would have been selfish enough to seek her out again. He didn't deserve Lucy.

But damn it, they were together again, and his guard had relaxed with each passing day. Hell, he'd spent the night at her house and instead of having nightmares, he'd slept better than he had since he'd entered the military. Images of casual Sunday nights at his parents, endless mornings waking next to Lucy, and a future without limits had filled him with hope.

Seeing her with one hand on some guy's arm, leaning in with her doe eyes wide, her expression serious, had slammed into him like a blow to the head. Maybe they'd moved forward too fast, fueled by sentiment from the "good old days" and it was time to hit the pause button. Or even turn off their movie for good this time.

There were other men out there who didn't have his issues--both physical and psychological--men who could give Lucy a life without all the baggage he carried. Although she'd broken off three engagements in their thirteen years apart and claimed to have always loved him.

His gut twisted, adding to the throbbing headache. Time to clear his head and stick these emotions back into the vault to contemplate later. His priority was Cypress Coast Ranch. Period.

His phone rang, time for a scheduled call with Austin, who wanted to discuss more specifics on the chef for the hotel's restaurant.

Cam massaged the iron muscles on the back of his neck, returned to his desk, and sat. God knows the distraction from the financial spreadsheets and obsessing over Lucy was a welcome one.

"Hey, is now still a good time to talk?" Austin Michaels' rock star voice rasped from the speaker phone on Cam's desk.

"Yeah, you're saving me from spreadsheet hell. How does Lucas stand working with this boring stuff all day?"

Austin snickered. "Right? I just pretend I don't understand and ask him so many questions that he does it for me. You should try it."

The pressure behind Cam's eyes relaxed and his lips quirked. Austin was always good for a laugh and damn good at getting his way. "Noted. So, what can I do for you?"

"It's what I can do for you, my friend."

"Yeah?" Cam leaned back in his chair and allowed his eyes to close.

"So, I was talking to Campbell, and we were discussing your parents' wedding and I thought it would be a great time to have the new chef come in and cater the meal. Kind of a soft opening for us at the restaurant. What do you think?"

Cam straightened. "I thought you were sold on this chef. Is something up?"

"No way. He's perfect. But why not, right? It will be a

great opportunity for him to meet the whole team, to see how he performs with a temporary kitchen, and it should be a fantastic brunch. Win-win."

"Sure." Cam sank back into his chair. "I can't believe my parents are getting married again."

Austin laughed. "Yeah, and guys like you and me never will. No ball and chains for us."

Something tightened in Cam's chest. Was he on track to spend his life with Lucy or to be alone? Sweat prickled between his shoulder blades. Until this morning he'd believed the former but maybe Austin was right.

"You still there?"

"Yeah, sorry." Cam rubbed the scruff on his jaw.

"Hmm…what's going on with you and the luscious Ms. Lucy?"

Cam's shoulders stiffened. "Don't call her that."

"Aha," Austin crowed. "I knew it. It's back on with you two, isn't it?"

Cam pinched the bridge of his nose. Maybe he needed another opinion and despite Austin's casual demeanor, he trusted his judgment. "Yeah, we've been seeing each other again."

"The tension between you two was intense last month at your parents'. Is it serious?"

Cam blew out a breath. "I'm crazy about her but I don't know if I'm what she needs." Understatement of the decade.

"Isn't that the attitude you had when you broke up with her all those years ago? Lucy strikes me as she knows her own mind and if she's with you now, it's because she wants to be. I like Lucy––she's probably the only one who can bring your cranky-ass self out of your shell." Austin's voice grew serious.

Cam rolled his eyes. "I'm not in a shell." *More like a damn porcupine, burrowed into its nest.* Except with the guys and his family. And Lucy.

"Whatever you say. Don't screw it up a second time, dude. But with you guys all getting hitched, I don't know if I want to open Palm Springs. Anyway, tell Lucy about the chef and I'll set up a call with her and Antonio. Gotta bolt." The line went dead.

Was Austin right? Cam glanced at his phone, which showed a few texts from Lucy. No way was he prepared to talk to her or see her today. Not yet. He needed some time to process the fire that had fueled through his veins when he saw her with her ex-fiancé. Damn, he'd hated seeing her with that guy. Imagining her beautiful brown eyes filled with emotion for someone other than him. Accepting his engagement ring.

But Lucy deserved a guy who didn't have trunks of baggage, like he did. She'd be better off without him. His gut clenched and he smacked his hands down on his desk.

Work. Time to compartmentalize and work. A few days to cool off would give him some perspective on whether it was time to end things with Lucy again. For good.

*L*ucy smoothed her hair back and checked her reflection in the mirror. She'd had a clothes crisis of epic proportions and now sweaters, jeans, and long-sleeved tops formed a giant mound on her bed. Give her a formal occasion or a casual outing and she was ready in ten minutes but to finally sit down and discuss the future with Cam––how could she decide?

She'd discarded a low-cut royal blue blouse because it was too sexy, like she was trying to seduce him into staying, although she was wearing matching red lace lingerie, just in case. One sweater looked frumpy, another like she was leaving for the slopes. She'd settled on a favorite pair of old jeans that were comfortable and made her butt look fabulous. A fitted black turtleneck was flattering without looking like she tried too hard. She hoped.

Her pulse skipped a beat when the doorbell rang. She checked the large vintage Paris clock above the stove––Cam was five minutes early, as usual. It had been a week since what she referred to as "the coffee shop incident." He'd asked for space and somehow, they'd managed to work together all that time and not run into each other. Evasion had always been one of his life skills.

She slicked on some rose-colored lip gloss and crossed to the door on wobbly legs. Go time.

When she opened the door, Cam stood framed in the doorway looking handsome and melancholy. His navy coat was open, revealing dark jeans and a fitted forest green sweater stretched across his sculpted chest and ridged abdominals. Frank sat at attention by his side, looking uncharacteristically solemn.

"Hi, come on in," she stepped aside. Frank galloped into her living room and skidded on the rug, his giant ears flopping.

"Frank," Cam said, shaking his head. "Sorry, I don't know if he'll ever grow any manners."

The dog loped back to Cam's side, leaned against him, and gazed up into his eyes.

Lucy laughed, grateful for the animal's ability to break the ice. "Manners are over-rated. That animal adores you."

Cam's lips twitched and he scratched behind Frank's ears. "Yeah, he's pretty great."

Lucy's breath regulated. So far so good. "What can I get you to drink? I've got some of that amber ale you like, and I've got a bottle of Barolo decanting."

"A beer would be good, thanks. And a bowl of water for him if that's not too much trouble." He remained rooted to the spot, as rigid as an on-duty sentry.

"Done. Give me a second. Take off your coat and have a seat." She crossed to the fridge, pulled out the beer bottle, and poured herself a healthy glass of the rich red wine.

Cam settled onto one side of the couch, she handed him the beer, and their fingers brushed, sparking a frisson of awareness up her arm. She retreated a step and sank into the other corner, tucking her legs beneath her. He seemed far away, the empty cushion between them like an invisible barrier.

Would tonight end how their relationship had thirteen years ago or be a new beginning? The silence yawned between them as they each sipped their drinks. Lucy huffed and set down her wineglass. They'd already wasted too much time and life was too short not to figure out if they were on or off. Enough.

"So, are you excited for your parents' ceremony next week?" Lucy asked. Start with an easy question to at least get them both talking.

Cam's lips quirked. "Yeah, my Mom is so excited. Hard not to get caught up in it all."

"Your dad, too. And I love that they're going on a mini honeymoon." Lucy's shoulders relaxed. "Your parents are really embracing their fresh start."

Her words hung in the air--maybe beginning their discussion with his parents was more strategic than she'd realized. Fresh starts all around.

He nodded, leaned forward, and set his beer on the coffee table. He massaged the back of his neck for a moment and blew out a heavy exhale. "I'm not good at this. I don't know what to say to you right now."

"Well how about answering the question if you're ready for a fresh start between us. It seemed like that's where we were headed and then you disappeared on me again." She kept her voice level, her expression neutral.

His crystalline eyes met hers. "I didn't disappear. I needed some time and we've both been busy."

"Okay, well it's been a week. Before that, everything was going great. Life is too short to be in limbo. I really need to know where your head is--correction, where your heart is. I love you Cam but I'm afraid you aren't ready to move forward. I'm afraid you'll never be ready to move forward."

Her nerves danced along her skin and her pulse kicked up in in her veins.

Cam dug his long fingers into his denim-clad thighs. "I needed time to think and whether you believe it or not, so did you. Seeing you with a guy you agreed to marry was tough."

Temper licked up her spine. "So, I was supposed to be single and pine away for you after you broke up with me?"

He held up one hand. "That's not what I'm saying. But it made me realize there are guys out there who you'd be better off marrying than me. Guys without the steamer trunks of baggage I've got. I'm not the same guy I was when we were together before."

She gasped and angled herself toward him fully. "No kidding. And I'm not the same woman--I've grown and changed too. What we had was real and what we have now is real. I would *not* be better off marrying someone I don't love the way I love you." *Not that he'd proposed.*

"I love you so much Lucy. You're the only woman I've ever loved." His brows drew together. "But I'm not the same man you fell in love with--war changed me and not just because I lost my leg. I don't want to let you down."

"Ohh." She hissed in frustration, leapt to her feet, and stalked across the room. "Well, I would think you would trust me to know my own heart and decide that. We're both the same people, we've just lived our lives. I see who you are now."

His ice blue eyes were bleak. "You asked how I feel and I'm telling you. I'm trying."

She closed her eyes and counted to five before looking at him again. "You're saying you don't believe me that I love all of you? Warts and all?"

He massaged his jaw and glanced down for a moment. "I

know you love me. I know we're good together. But I'm damaged and I don't want to hold you back."

A thread of vulnerability laced his gravelly voice. A sign he was insecure about her true feelings. The anger immediately fell away and she returned to the couch. She sank down next to him and caught his broad hands in hers.

"Cam." She searched his gaze. "Take marriage out of the equation for a minute. I'll tell you the reasons I want to be with you now, the reasons why you've always held my heart even after all the years, and why I know I'm right about us.

"I love how brave and confident you are, I love that you're a born leader. I love your sense of honor and loyalty and duty, not just to your family and your friends but to our country. You're easy on the eyes and our chemistry is once in a lifetime. You're responsible, passionate, but you're also grumpy, bossy, aloof, and a stubborn pain in the butt."

He'd intertwined his fingers with hers, his pale blue eyes gleaming. "Hey, I'm not bossy."

Her lips quirked. "Yes, you are. That's why you were a great leader and why you're great running Cypress Coast Ranch. And thanks for not arguing about being a pain in the butt."

His clenched jaw softened, and he flashed his white teeth. "Takes one to know one. Do you really mean all of that?"

"Of course, I mean it." She waved her hands in the air. "Part of my heart was always yours and when you returned, all that love blossomed again, and the truth is that my whole heart belongs to you."

His eyes lit up and in a swift move, he pulled her onto his lap, and wrapped his powerful arms around her. He slid one hand up to cradle the back of her head and leaned his forehead against hers. She traced her fingertips up to his muscular chest and pressed her palm against his heart. His breath caught and his heartbeat thundered beneath her touch.

They remained that way, breathing each other in. The heat from his skin mingled with hers, his clean masculine scent filled her senses, and Lucy melted into his possessive embrace.

He shifted back a few inches, far enough to gaze into her eyes. "It's always been you, Lucy. Only you. I screwed up when I left you that way. I was immature, I was afraid I'd screw up my career and our relationship. We can't change the past, but we can start fresh. And it's my turn to tell you why I love you and how sorry I am."

Her pulse was racing, and warmth suffused her skin. "You've apologized and I know you mean it. But feel free to tell me why you love me."

His arms banded tighter around her, and his lips twitched. "First, let me finish my apology––I know I'm slow to process my emotions. I shouldn't have made you wait so long but I'm a total idiot. Everything's changed so much in my life and it's all great but sometimes it's hard for me to trust that I deserve to have it all. Deserve you."

Her eyes blurred and she blinked. "Cam, I love you so much, even when you're an idiot. And you do deserve to have an amazing life."

His cerulean eyes lit up. "I promise you can trust me––I'll never leave you again. I want to have an amazing life with you and I'm going to do better." He lowered his mouth to hers in a tender kiss.

"We can do better together. But about that loving me part?" She waved a hand. "Proceed."

Cam grinned. "I love what a smart-ass you can be. I love how you always see the best in people, how optimistic and smart you are. I love your compassion and friendliness, and genuine caring for others. I love how you are sweet and gracious but have the most resilient, strong character I've ever known. Tons of people claim they value every moment of life but you're one of the few people I know who lives that way. You're just as much of a stubborn pain in the butt as me but you're so gorgeous I'll take the trade-off."

He captured her mouth. Her lips parted and she deepened the kiss, savoring his unique flavor and the dancing of their tongues.

Cam gripped her hips and shifted them so she could straddle him.

Frank woofed and leapt up from the floor, where he'd been napping by Cam's feet. Lucy giggled and scooted toward the middle of the couch. "I think Frank approves."

Cam grinned. "Yeah, he seems to read my moods. But then again, I think he may need to go outside. Give me a second." He rose from the couch and signaled for the dog to follow him to the front door.

Lucy picked up her wine and sipped. Joy spread through her being––she and Cam were figuring their relationship out and she had faith they would build a beautiful life together.

He returned with Frank, who galloped in and promptly placed his shaggy head on her leg. "This boy is shameless in his drive for attention." She laughed and rubbed the dog's velvety fur.

Cam reached out one hand and helped her to her feet. "Definitely. But he's ready to go to bed and so am I. Can I stay with you tonight?"

Heat curled down her spine. "I'd love that. Does Frank need anything before we go to my room?"

"He's got water and he'll be fine sleeping out here." He pulled her against his lean muscular frame.

She gazed up at Cam with a wicked grin. "Great because I wore something special tonight and I think you'll need all your attention to enjoy."

"Oh really?" His brows flew up and his pupils flared.

She winked. "Oh really. Come with me."

He bent down, scooped her into his arms, and brushed his lips over hers and murmured, "Did I mention I love your sexy little body, too?"

A spear of heat shot straight to her center. "And I love your big strong one. Let me show you how much." She turned her head and pressed a kiss to his smiling mouth.

In three long strides, they reached her bedroom where they had all night to show each other just how much.

EPILOGUE #1

Taylors' Vow Renewal Ceremony
  Cypress Coast Ranch--April

Lucy's heels clicked on the gravel path beneath her feet and the salty breeze kissed her cheeks beneath the soft rays of morning sunshine. The marine layer was fading from the horizon, revealing streaks of cornflower blue sky and hints of a perfect day for the Taylors' vow renewal ceremony. She scanned the garden venue, nodding in approval at the neat rows of chairs with their lavender and white chiffon bows fluttering in the chilly air. She muttered a silent prayer that the temperature rose at least five degrees by 11:30, so the wedding party wouldn't be forced to wear their coats.

"It looks incredible out here, my mom is going to be thrilled." Cam's low voice rasped.

She turned and her breath caught. The breeze blew the fabric of his crisp white shirt against him, revealing his broad chest and defined abs. He'd opted not to wear a tie and she ached to press her lips to the tanned hollow of his throat.

"You look incredible, and I'm thrilled." Goosebumps prickled along her skin and not from the cool morning.

His lips quirked up. "Do you have a few minutes to take a walk with me before everyone begins arriving?" He slid his arms around her, lowered his head and brushed his mouth against hers.

She tilted her head back and wound her arms around his neck. "I do." She clung to his broad shoulders, his powerful physique her anchor. "I'm just so happy to help your parents celebrate. And it will be a blast to see everyone."

"It will." He stepped back, reached for her hand, and started toward the hotel's private beach. The gravel path turned to sand and crunched beneath their feet, the large winter surf crashed in the distance, and the cry of seagulls punctuated the morning air.

When they reached the cove, Cam stopped and wrapped one muscular arm around her, drawing her to his side. She slipped her arm around his narrow waist and leaned her head against him. For a few minutes, they watched the waves breaking on the beach. Joy filled her. They'd settled into a slow and steady rhythm with busy days at work and passionate nights at home. Savoring each day as it arrived, just like she'd hoped and dreamed.

She tilted her head up and smiled. "Are you nervous about giving your mom away to your dad? I can give you some pointers, seeing as I'm a wedding expert and all."

His lips twitched. "I think I can handle that part. But how today goes depends on you."

"Me?"

Cam turned toward her and grasped both of her hands. His crystal blue eyes gazed into her own, his pupils dilating. "Yes you, Lucy Goodwin."

Her heart kicked against her ribs and her mouth went Palm Springs Desert dry.

Cam kept her hands clasped in his. His face grew serious, his square jaw tight, his eyes gleaming. "From the first moment I saw you in high school, you took my breath away. In that moment, I knew you were the one for me, even though we were teenagers. You are the sweetest, most compassionate, resilient person I've ever met. I don't know how I got so lucky as to get a second chance with you after making the biggest mistake of my life, but here we are.

"Since the moment I saw you outside the conference room, you reawakened my heart and made me want to feel again. To live again. To be the best man I can be. You're the perfect woman for me and I'm far from perfect but I promise you I'll spend the rest of my life showing you how much I love you. Will you marry me?"

Lucy's heart burst with joy and she threw her arms around his neck. "Yes, yes, yes! I love you so much Cameron Taylor. I think you're perfect exactly how you are. I would be thrilled to be your wife."

He lowered his head and captured her mouth in a passionate kiss. She melted against his hard, hot body and savored his strength. He lifted his head and she moaned in protest. "More kisses please."

His laugh was light and free. "Hold on a minute."

He stepped back and reached into the pocket of his charcoal gray slacks and pulled out a small velvet box. He flipped open the lid, revealing a canary yellow diamond flanked by delicate clear diamonds in an old-fashioned platinum setting. "Let's make it official."

She gasped at the way the sunlight glinted off the unique ring. "It's so beautiful." She held out her hand and he slipped the ring on her finger.

"How did you know I loved yellow diamonds? It's perfect. I love you."

He grinned. "Don't laugh but I remember you and Campbell making a huge deal out of Victoria Beckham's ring when she married David Beckham. You said something like you had to have one."

Lucy threw back her head and laughed. "I cannot believe you remember that, but yes, I have always thought they were so gorgeous."

He hugged her close and she leaned into his tall muscular frame. "Today is one of the best days of my life. And my mom is going to be thrilled when we tell her."

Lucy tilted her head. "Usually, I advise guests not to get engaged at their relatives' weddings but in this case, I think you're right. Your parents are going to be really happy. But let's wait until after the ceremony to say anything. Okay?"

Cam nodded and lowered his forehead against hers. "You're the expert. Whatever you say."

She grinned and shifted to press her lips against his. "I like the sound of that."

"I bet you do," he murmured and stroked his hands down her spine. "Are you ready to head up to the hotel so we're there to greet the guests?"

Tingles traveled from the soles of her feet and spiraled up her spine. "Let's do this."

Hands intertwined, they strolled up the winding path toward the rest of their lives.

EPILOGUE #2

Cypress Coast Ranch Opening Gala––May

Lucy's lips curved up in satisfaction as she surveyed the lively well-dressed crowd gathered in the expansive ballroom and spilling out into Cypress Coast Ranch's gardens. Strands of twinkling lights glittered along the open floor-to-ceiling doors and soft jazz music from the band playing outside filled the air. Servers wove through the throngs, offering flutes of champagne and savory hors d'oeuvres.

She turned and looped her arms around Cam's strong neck, rose on her tiptoes, and pressed a featherlight kiss against his lips. "Everything is perfect. You pulled off tonight's opening like a veteran hotel exec."

"You're perfect. I couldn't have done it without you." His crystal blue eyes gleamed under the golden glow from the ballroom's chandeliers. "I love you so much."

Contentment filled her being. "I love you Cam. Forever."

"Do you think anyone would notice if we snuck off for a few minutes?" He winked.

She giggled. "Um, yeah. The entire Hotel King team is

making a beeline for us right now. Remember, you're on the hook for giving the speech to all the guests."

Cam slid one arm around her and hugged her close to his lean muscular body. "Ryan or Jack should do that," he said with a groan.

Ryan and Charlie, Jack and Campbell, Austin, Lucas, and their assistant Jon joined them. "Ryan or Jack should do what?" Austin, looking handsome in a dark suit, asked.

"Give the welcome speech. Or you could do it--practice for opening Palm Springs in October," Cam said.

Austin threw back his head and laughed. "Nice try. If you two can stop making out for a few minutes, all you need to do is give a toast. Say welcome and thank you."

Cam rolled his eyes. "We weren't making out. Fine, I'll give the toast. But don't ask for help when it's your turn."

"For the guy who accused me of making the Maison du Soleil opening like a Hallmark movie of the week, I'd think you'd be more discreet at your hotel's opening." Jack smirked.

Campbell swatted her big brother's shoulder. "Exactly. And here you are looking just like the happy couple at the end of the movie. Thank you, Lucy, for helping to expose Cam's true colors."

Lucy leaned her head against Cam's broad shoulder and grinned. "Happy to oblige. And let's get the toast out of the way so we can celebrate."

"Raise your glasses everyone. Time for a toast." Austin raised his glass high and used his lead singer pipes to quiet the room. The conversations muted.

He turned to Cam with a crooked grin. "Don't say I never did anything for you."

Cam cleared his throat and lifted his champagne in the air. "Don't worry, I'm not going to give a long speech. On behalf of the Hotel Kings, I want to thank you for joining us tonight to commemorate the grand opening of Monterey Peninsula's newest luxury resort. Enjoy your evening and we hope to see you here again soon. Cheers."

"Cheers." The clinking of glasses and clapping of hands filled the room.

"Great job, Cam. You too, Lucy. Everything is going better than we could have envisioned," Ryan smiled.

"Thanks. It's been an amazing ride and so much more than I could have hoped." Cam gazed down at Lucy, a tender smile on his square-jawed face.

Lucy's heart squeezed with joy. "I'd say so. And now it's Austin's turn to find his true love."

Austin retreated a step, his dark brows drawn together. "Um, no. It's my turn to open the next hotel. Just because you all are wrapped up in this wedding stuff doesn't mean I'm interested. Back me up, Lucas and Jon."

Jon, who worked for Ryan and Charlie in La Jolla, snickered. "Don't look at me. I'm still waiting for the man of my dreams to sweep me off my feet."

"I wouldn't be so sure, dude. Have you seen the woman who's interviewing to run the spa at your hotel yet?" Lucas asked, his eyes wide behind his wire-rimmed glasses.

Austin shook his head. "We've spoken on the phone and are meeting next week in the desert. Mackenzie's here?"

Lucas discreetly pointed toward the open doorway to the patio and gardens. "Charlie invited her so she could meet everyone. She's the redhead in the lacy white dress."

Austin whistled under his breath and took a pull from his beer. "Damn, she's a knock-out."

Charlie winked at Lucy before turning to Austin. "She's got an incredible reputation for creating the most popular and lucrative spa programs in the country and even internationally. She's a master yoga instructor and is all about creating healing, tranquil spaces. She's perfect for Palm Springs."

Ryan barked out a laugh. "Yeah, because my baby brother is so Zen. Can you imagine him inviting her on a motorcycle ride to some alt-rock dive bar?"

Lucy frowned. "Don't make assumptions about either of them. I mean, opposites attract is one of the most popular tropes in all those romance movies. Austin, it is your turn after all. You should go ask Mackenzie to dance or at least introduce yourself."

Austin shook his head. "I'm going to find my parents––at least they aren't trying to marry me off. I'll meet her later." He pivoted on his heel and bolted in the opposite direction.

For a moment, nobody spoke.

"Who wants to put twenty down that Austin falls for the yoga teacher?" Jack asked, his green eyes alight with mischief.

"Wouldn't that be fun to watch? I'm in. Let's toast to Austin." Lucy grinned.

Everyone laughed and raised their glasses. Love and hotel openings were apparently a thing.

WHAT'S NEXT

Thank you for reading *Monterey King*! I hope you loved Cameron and Lucy's story as much as I loved writing it.

If you have a moment, please leave a review for **Monterey King** on your favorite book site.

****

Ready for Austin to meet his match, Mackenzie? **Palm Springs King** is available now!

ACKNOWLEDGMENTS

As always, writing a book is a team effort! This past year was a challenging one for me on a personal level and I struggled to get the words on the page. I couldn't have finished Cam and Lucy's story without all the patient assistance I received.

I want to thank my wonderful beta readers: Joanna Kelly, Sara Martin, Kay Bennett, Donna Simonetta, and my brother Robert Petretti—your individualized feedback helped me shape the final version of the story more than you could imagine. I appreciate your time and opinions. Thank you so much to Mallnee Mitchell for your insider info on Monterey and being an overall awesome human! Big thanks to Lisa Ray for sharing your hotel industry expertise (again.) Any errors in the book are mine. Thank you to Brenda St. John Brown for helping me write the blurb (again!)

For the lovely author friends I've made along the way, with whom I share such a sense of camaraderie, thanks for being there, through thick and thin. You know who you are!

To my wonderful editor, Lindsey Faber, thank you for your brilliance! I don't know how I finished books before you and I know you went above and beyond for this story. Thank you to Shasta Shafer for her excellent proofreading. Thank you, Christina Hovland, for this gorgeous cover-- you are one talented woman and caring friend.

Last but not least, to Todd for your unwavering belief in me. I love you. And, finally to my furry kids: Lola, Beau, Josie, and Daisy, thanks for providing me daily laughs and all the cuddles.

ABOUT THE AUTHOR

Claire Marti is an award winning and *USA Today* Bestselling author of swoonworthy Contemporary Romance novels set in Southern California, including the Pacific Vista Ranch series and spin-off California Suits series. She lives in San Diego with her husband, silly dog and three clever cats.

Claire started writing stories as soon as she was old enough to pick up pencil and paper. After graduating from the University of Virginia with a BA in English Literature, Claire was sidetracked by other careers, including practicing law, selling software for legal publishers, and managing a non-profit animal rescue for a Hollywood actress.

Finally, Claire followed her heart and now focuses on two of her true passions: writing romance and teaching yoga.